Love's Compass
Book Four
Finding Faith

Melanie D. Snitker

" Faith is being sure of
what we hope for and
certain of " what we
do not see. " Hebrews 11:1

MDSnitker

2-9-16

For our amazing son, Xander.
You are a mighty warrior and
I couldn't be more proud of you.
I love you!

CONTENTS

CONTENTS

Chapter One
Mid-June

Serenity Chandler scanned the headlines displayed on the various magazines in the checkout line. Most were so outrageous, she had no desire to flip through the pages. A cooking title caught her eye. Fancy summer cakes shaped like watermelons and flowers decorated the cover. Beautiful? Yes. Did she have time to bake something that detailed? Absolutely not.

Even if she did, she'd probably cringe the first time she had to cut into it. Nope, the extent of her baking this summer would be opening up a box of Hostess cakes and calling it a day.

They inched forward and stopped next to the candy display. Gideon grabbed her hand and pulled on it.

"What is it, big guy?" He pointed to the orange Tic Tacs sitting above his head. Serenity picked up a container and handed it to him. "You have to wait until we get back to the car to eat them, though."

He cupped the candy in his hands and smiled brightly. She wondered if her son was the only five-

1

year-old who would happily pass up the vast selection of chocolate for one little box of orange mints. He certainly didn't get that from her.

The woman in front of her placed a dozen or more cans of soup on the conveyor belt before turning to her. "Too much chocolate, not enough time, huh?"

Serenity blinked at her. "Yeah. Something like that." She might have been tempted to choose a chocolate bar for herself. Heaven knew she could use one. But the woman in front of her must have used half a bottle of perfume. The musk tangoed with the scent of meatloaf and gravy that Serenity had spilled on her uniform at work. The combination didn't exactly elicit a desire to eat chocolate or anything else.

She scratched at the skin beneath the collar of her shirt. It would have been nice if she could've changed before going to the store. As it was, she was glad she'd made it to the school in time to pick Gideon up from his special needs program. Now, if she could get through this line and out again before breakfast tomorrow, that would be a wonderful bonus.

By the time Serenity reached the cashier, she was so ready to get out of the store, her legs ached. "Put your candy up there, Gideon."

He did as she asked, staying beside it as their groceries moved towards the guy scanning their items.

Once she got the grocery cart situated near the bags, Serenity positioned her debit card above the reader, prepared to slide it through. Small hands grabbed her elbow, the card missing its mark. She took in a deep breath and glanced down at Gideon.

He tugged on her elbow again and emphatically pointed to the red exit sign on the electronic door. A desperate look filled his brown eyes.

"I know, big guy. We're almost done." She just started sliding her card again when another tug brought her arm down. If possible, Gideon's eyes were even wider. She took his hand and placed it on the handle of the shopping cart. "Five more minutes. Keep your hand on the basket, please."

Her third attempt worked and Serenity waited for the machine to show the payment was being processed. She bounced on the balls of her feet as sweat followed a path between her shoulder blades and down her back. It never mattered what time of the year it was, this grocery store was always too hot. Management could afford to repair the air conditioner with the money she spent there alone. She ought to start shopping at the store across town. That'd show them.

Who was she kidding? She shopped here because she knew the layout and it was close to home. The last thing she had time for was navigating an unknown store.

She ruffled Gideon's hair. If his flushed cheeks turned any redder, they'd match the shirt he was wearing. She couldn't blame him for being impatient, especially when she had to hold the record for picking the world's longest checkout line. She stared at the display on the card reader, releasing a breath when the transaction completed.

The cashier gave Gideon a kind smile. "I don't like going shopping, either." The boy said nothing. The cashier handed the long receipt to Serenity. "Not very talkative, is he?"

Too exhausted to go into an explanation of how her son had autism and was non-verbal, Serenity put a hand on either side of Gideon's. "No, he isn't. Thank you." Together, they pushed the basket away from the checkout.

"You're welcome, have a great day."

"You too." The cashier probably didn't hear her, but the need to escape the confines of the store took precedence. Gideon used one hand to fish around in a plastic bag for his candy while the other pointed to the exit sign. "Absolutely. Let's get out of here."

It was funny how the June Texas heat felt less stifling than the recycled air they left behind in the store. She breathed deeply, welcoming the hot breeze.

Pushing the basket down a row of cars, she watched Gideon hop from oil spot to oil spot as if he were using stepping stones to traverse a creek. There was a time when she tried to convince him that the oil only made his shoes dirty. Now she appreciated the expression of contentment on his face.

Normally, after his special needs program at the local school, he was stressed and moody. He only went twice a week, but it was enough to make her dread sending him to school full time in the fall. She had a gut feeling public school wasn't going to be a good fit for him. For the hundredth time that summer, she wished she had the money to get him into a good private school. Somewhere he would thrive.

Once reaching their car, Serenity held the button on her key remote until the trunk clicked open. She loaded the groceries and then settled Gideon into his five-point harness. She brushed the dark hair out of his eyes. "I love you, big guy."

~

Serenity stretched her legs and shifted in the chair on the backyard patio. The sun warmed her skin as she watched Gideon scoop sand and pour it into an ever-growing pile.

The sound of the screen door opening dragged Serenity's attention from the notepad on her lap to her sister. Lexi closed it again behind her and sank into a second patio chair nearby.

"Hey! Did you just get here?"

Lexi motioned towards the house with her thumb. "I had some coupons to drop off for Grams. I figured I'd do that on the way home."

"I'm sure she appreciated it. Where's your significant other?"

"Lance is at the workshop. He said he had to finish staining a set of bunk beds before he could head home tonight. I figured I may as well come by and say hi."

"I'm surprised that new husband of yours is even letting you out of his sight." Serenity winked at her.

Lexi rolled her eyes, but the smile on her face showed how content she was. Serenity enjoyed seeing it. After Lexi's battle with cancer the previous fall, she deserved every bit of happiness she got.

Gideon observed them and Lexi waved at him. "What are you up to?"

Serenity held up her pad. "Just making a to-do list for this coming week."

Lexi threw her a slightly disapproving glare, the kind only big sisters can manage. "And here I thought you were out here relaxing for a change."

A short bark of a laugh escaped Serenity's throat. Relax? This was as close as she came to that. As it was, she was struggling to keep her eyes open long enough to get through dinner and make it to bedtime.

Her exhaustion must have shone on her face because Lexi's own filled with concern. "It's not good for you to be this stressed out."

"I know." Serenity reached over to gently finger the short strands that barely covered the tips of Lexi's ears. "It's getting longer. I think it might be a little lighter than it was before." Watching Lexi lose her hair during the cancer treatments had hit the whole family hard.

Lexi's head bobbed. "I think so, too." She ran a hand over the short-cropped hair. "I'm glad it's finally growing back. Going through winter with a bald head was an interesting experience. I'll be happy to not repeat that again."

Serenity pulled some of her waist-length hair around to her chest. "I'm tempted to cut mine. I'm ready for a change."

"Are we talking about your hair? Or something else?"

Serenity threw her a glare. Lexi was way too good at picking up the subtleties. She thought about redirecting the conversation. Instead, she shifted and withdrew a pamphlet from her back pocket. "Maybe both." She handed it over.

Lexi took in the "Hope Academy" title across the top. Her eyes widened as she scanned over the information. "This school's in the Dallas area. Are you considering it for Gideon?"

Serenity had been ever since she received the pamphlet in the mail a few weeks ago. How the special needs private school got her name and address in the first place, she didn't know. After nearly throwing it away several times, Serenity had finally sat down and read through it. Everything about the school sounded like a Godsend for Gideon — from the student-led curriculum schedule to the music, speech, and occupational therapies.

There was no way she would be able to afford something like this, though. And that had kept her from even giving them a call. Until the other day.

Serenity shrugged. "Possibly. It's a long shot, but they have scholarships. And an administrative job opening." She threw a cautious glance at the back door. This was not a conversation she was ready to have with Mom or Grams. Not yet. "Every time I try to let the idea go, I feel like God brings it to mind again. I think I'm going to apply for the scholarships and send in my resume. Insane, right?"

Her stomach was a bundle of nerves as she watched Lexi digest her words. She fully expected to hear all the reasons why she shouldn't even think about it. How moving away from Kitner and her family would be a mistake.

With her elbows on her knees, Lexi studied Serenity as if she were trying to diagnose one of her pediatric patients. "Are you content with your life?"

What kind of question was that? "I have the best kid in the world and I'm close to all of my family. I don't really have anything to complain about."

"That's not what I asked you. Are you content with where you are in your life right now?"

Serenity sank into the nylon backing of her chair and released a breath. "No. I hate my job, Lexi. Some days, it's all I can do to walk into that restaurant. And the thought of Gideon going to Powell — that school is going to eat him alive." Imagining her son falling through the cracks brought tears to her eyes. "I sometimes feel like I'm stuck in a hole that just keeps getting deeper and deeper."

Lexi tapped the brochure with a finger. "Then perhaps this is God's way of throwing you a ladder so you can climb back out. Look, you allow yourself to stay shackled to things in the past. To Jay and everything that happened between the two of you. And it isn't right. You deserve to be happy. If it takes making a drastic change in your life before you find that happiness, then so be it."

Serenity let the words wash over her. Maybe — just maybe — a new beginning was what she needed. "It doesn't hurt to send the application and resume, right?"

With a mischievous wink, Lexi crossed one ankle over her knee and grinned. "No, it certainly doesn't."

Chapter Two
End of July

Serenity shoved a box with her foot and sucked in a sharp breath when it didn't move an inch. A zap of pain raced up her leg. Performing what she was sure could pass as a circus act, she managed not to drop the box she was carrying. She set it down on the bed and joined it, massaging her calf. Good grief, the last thing she needed was to break a toe less than two weeks before she started her new job. Not to mention she had no idea where the closest ER was in her new neighborhood near Dallas.

"Are you okay?"

Serenity let her foot fall to the floor and gazed up to find Tuck studying her closely. He was obviously in full big brother mode.

"Yes, I'm fine. I stubbed my toe."

"I'm sorry to hear that. But I'm not talking about your foot."

Sounds of other family members carrying boxes into the new rental house floated through the door.

Serenity gave Tuck what she hoped was her best, "Don't even start" expression. "We've talked about this until we've both been blue in the face. I'm fine. This is the best thing for Gideon right now. And me, too."

"Moving away from your family?"

A heavy sigh worked its way from her lungs. "No. Moving towards a new opportunity. This special needs school is huge for Gideon. He needs it. And I need a change of scenery. It's time I did something on my own."

Tuck folded his arms and leaned against the wall. His brows knit together and if he stared at her any harder, she wouldn't have been surprised if he could have heard her thoughts. Just when she expected him to start lecturing her, his expression softened. "I *am* proud of you. What you're doing — it can't be easy."

"It's not." When Serenity had sent in the application, she hadn't really expected Gideon to receive a scholarship. Not long after giving up, she heard back from the school and learned, not only had he been accepted, but the scholarship he qualified for covered a surprising seventy-five percent of Gideon's tuition. She was still amazed every time she thought about it. Getting a job at the same school further assured her that the move was a good one.

She was going to make it work and her family didn't need to know she might not have much left after paying tuition and rent. Not when they'd practically thrown an intervention to keep her from moving. With the exception of Lexi, who insisted that a new beginning might be exactly what Serenity needed.

She planted her hands on her hips and stared at Tuck. "I'm less than three hours away. You come up here on cases semi-regularly. And we'll make it down for the weekend here and there."

Tuck straightened, switching from big brother to cop mode. "You'll call if you need anything."

It wasn't a question. Serenity suppressed a smile. Her brother would protect her no matter what. "I will. I promise."

He gave a firm nod. "We'll come visit, too. Once Laurie's feeling better. This pregnancy has her getting sick just from driving from our house to her studio." A wave of sympathy passed over his face. "I can't imagine what a drive like this would do to her. She felt bad for not helping you move."

Serenity didn't blame her sister-in-law. She remembered well how close she and the toilet had become after dealing with morning sickness while carrying Gideon. She didn't envy Laurie one bit. "Please tell her not to feel bad. Growing another human being's a lot of work."

Lance peeked his blond head around the corner, his eyes full of mischief. "If you guys are done with your little work-avoiding pow-wow, could you tell me where you want me to put these miscellaneous boxes?"

Serenity stood, relieved that her foot no longer hurt. She led her brother-in-law into the living room. "Anywhere in here is fine. Those are the boxes that I'm going to have to find a home for."

Grams spoke from her spot on the futon. "If you run out of room and you need us to keep anything for you, we'll be happy to."

Mom nodded her agreement. Her eyes were misty. She'd been emotional for the better part of the last couple of weeks. Serenity flashed her a quick smile of thanks but averted her own eyes quickly. Tears were already threatening to spill and she didn't need that. Not now.

Lance placed the box he was holding against a wall and dusted his hands off on his pants. "I think that's the last one."

"Nope." Lexi emerged with another box in her arms. "This is, though." She set it down on top of the one Lance was carrying and moved to stand next to him. He pulled her closer with one arm and kissed her on the temple.

Serenity suddenly felt like everyone was staring at her. And no one was saying a word. She cleared her throat, the sound echoing off the walls. "You guys are the best. Thank you all so much." She wanted to say more, but the words lodged in her throat. How did she tell her family goodbye? She'd reminded Tuck she was only a few hours away, but it seemed like much more right now.

Footsteps approached them from one of the two bedrooms and Gideon threw himself into the recliner. He relaxed, his legs stretched across one of the arms while his head rested on the other. A huge smile lit his face, eliciting chuckles from around the room.

Tuck went forward and ruffled the boy's hair. "We're going to miss you both."

His words about did Serenity in. Since Gideon's father had been absent from his life since day one, Tuck had been that influencing figure for him. She felt worse about separating the two of them than she did anything else.

Grams pushed herself up off the futon. "That's enough of this pity party. The longer we stand here waiting to see who starts crying first, the harder it's going to be." Even as she said the words, a tear trickled from the corner of her eye. No one was about to point it out and more than one sniffle from somewhere else in the room followed in its wake.

Mom's eyes got wide and she looked from Grams to Serenity. "We can help you unpack. I hate bringing all your things in and just leaving."

The family had gone into town earlier, had a leisurely take-out lunch at the new house, and then started unloading the truck. Serenity didn't know where she wanted anything to go, much less tell anyone else. As much as she didn't want them to go, anything else was prolonging the inevitable.

Lexi squeezed Lance's hand. "Grams is right, Mom. We need to leave if we're going to get back before dark. And I think Serenity probably could use some time to figure out where she wants everything."

Serenity bobbed her head. She picked at the hem of her shirt, attempting to distract herself from the tears that were building. Again. She looked around the room at the faces of her family. They'd supported her and Gideon for so long. Could she make it without them? Right now, she wasn't sure. The little girl in her didn't want to find out. She wanted to go back to the Chandler house, safe with Mom and Grams.

But that was the problem, right? She was safe there. And stuck. She had to do something for herself and her son and this was the first step. Even if it was a doozy.

Her eyelashes fluttered, her last defense against the tears. "I've got this. I'll probably tackle it throughout the week. You guys helped with the hardest part."

There was another round of silence before everyone gravitated towards the middle of the room. When the first set of arms circled Serenity, the tears broke through. She didn't even try to stop them. Instead, they painted evidence of her mixed emotions as they slid down her cheeks.

After countless whispers of "I love you" and "We'll see you soon," Serenity stood on the front porch of their little two-bedroom duplex with Gideon's hand in hers. She waved both of their hands as she watched the caravan of vehicles disappear from view.

She swiped at the tears and ignored the headache that was quickly gaining momentum. When Serenity turned, she found Gideon's eyes on her.

"I'm okay, big guy. It's just hard to say goodbye." She planted a kiss on the back of his hand before releasing it. "What do you say we unpack your room and get it all set up?"

Gideon pulled open the screen door so quickly that it hit the side of the house before Serenity could stop it. He was already running down the short hallway when she stepped inside.

Taking in the cluttered room full of boxes, she released a steadying breath. "Well, God, we did it. Please help us all as we adjust." She said an extra prayer for Gideon. He was excited now, but she wasn't sure how well he was going to sleep in a new house. Hopefully getting his room set up would help.

She also prayed he'd like the new school a lot more than he'd liked his previous program. The thought shifted towards her own first day at Hope Academy. Everyone there had seemed nice enough when she'd gone for her interview. But what if she didn't get along with her co-workers? Her family had served as her friends for a long time. She prayed she'd be able to make a friend or two once she got settled in.

~

Aaron Randall performed a visual tour of his classroom, making sure everything was in its place. This was the last of the two-week summer break before all of the children came back to Hope Academy on Monday. He'd finished cleaning the tables and instruments that morning. Printouts and activities were ready for the new school year.

A light knocking at the doorway drew his attention. Letty, a kindergarten teacher and one of his friends, walked in and motioned towards the large keyboard rug in the middle of the room. "I heard you found a new one. That's fantastic."

Aaron smiled at the rainbow-colored keys. When he saw it in a catalog, he knew it had to go in his music room. "Think the kids are going to like it?"

Letty lifted an eyebrow. "Definitely. Though you may have a hard time with Cecil focusing on anything but that when he walks in."

He laughed. He had to admit the boy had been the first to come to mind when he saw the rug. Cecil had a love for everything related to the piano.

Letty's expression sobered. "Did you get the memo?"

Aaron resisted the urge to roll his eyes. The page-long memo had been delivered to every teacher, therapist, and member of the administration. There was nothing like a heading of "New Policy Regarding Dating" to snag his attention.

He hooked a thumb through one of his belt loops and leaned against a table. "You mean the one suggesting that, if anyone working here gets involved with the parent of a student, they may be fired?"

"Yeah. I thought it was a little harsh."

Aaron thought so, too. After the whole fiasco with one of the teachers at Hope Academy going out with a student's mom and breaking up in the middle of the hallway, everyone anticipated some kind of response from the board of directors. But the memo did seem a bit overdone.

"I do get how it put the powers that be in a bad position. But I think it would've all blown over. This school has been in place for fifteen years. If that's the first time it's happened, we're doing pretty well."

Letty lifted her left hand and wiggled her fingers, the lights reflecting off her wedding ring. "I'm glad I found my man before all of this happened."

"I doubt you'd have gotten in trouble for going out with the computer tech." He and Zane had been friends for over two years before the couple had started dating. The romance between the two couldn't have been more perfect — or entertaining.

She shrugged. "Maybe not. But at least we don't have to worry about it." She jerked a thumb towards the door. "Speaking of the hubby, we're supposed to go to lunch. You want to join us?"

"I appreciate it. But I think I'm going to finish up here and then stop by the music store this afternoon."

"Sounds good. See you later."

Aaron waved his goodbye. He had to admit there were times when he envied their relationship. To have someone to go home to, or even hang out with, was something he hoped to experience himself one day.

But for now, all he had waiting for him was his forty-inch television and a recliner with his name on it.

He'd just dropped off a few things in the mailroom when Cynthia, one of the assistant directors, peeked her head around the corner. "Can I talk to you for a minute?"

Oh, great. The only time she wanted to talk to him was if she needed his help or wanted to remind him to do something. He shoved down his annoyance when he really wished he'd seen her in time to duck into another room. "What's up?"

"Did you get the memo?"

"Yes. I found it in my box when I got in this morning."

"Good. Do you have any questions about the new guidelines?"

Was she serious? If it were anyone else, he would have joked. *I know my students' mothers are out of the question. What if one of them has a hot sister? Is that against the new guidelines?* He could imagine the vein in her temple nearly popping through the skin. It took a lot of willpower to keep the grin off his face.

"Not a one. Is there a reason why you're concerned?"

"I'm checking in with everyone." She gave him a dismissive flick of her head. "Have a great afternoon."

Who did the woman think she was kidding? Everyone had seen the guidelines and she didn't need to treat them all like children. Maggie and Rachelle, one in administration and one who worked in the lunchroom, flirted with the guys more than about any other women he'd been around. He'd gotten to where he made a point of not being alone with either of them. But even then, he highly doubted they would go against the policy, either.

Cynthia certainly didn't have to worry about Aaron. The only thing he could afford to focus on was teaching his students and his music.

Chapter Three

Serenity strained her neck until she could see Gideon's face in the rearview mirror. "What do you think, big guy? Are we ready?" He pointed at the large brick building with "Hope Academy" on a plaque above the oversized double doors. "Okay, let's go do this."

It was Thursday and they had an appointment to come by before school started on Monday. A couple of weeks ago, they went in for her interview and an evaluation for Gideon. Now, they wanted to show her a little about what she'd be doing and have her fill out some of the other forms — primarily health insurance. They'd assured her that one of the teachers would take Gideon and let him play in the gym while she did so.

Her nerves rolled around in her stomach like pool balls and she swiped her sweaty palms against her pants as they got out of the car.

They walked hand-in-hand to one of the large doors and opened it together. She led Gideon towards the long desk where parents were supposed to check in. A woman looked up and smiled brightly, her head full of tight, red curls bouncing as she moved. Serenity guessed they were around the same age. "Good morning. Can I help you?"

"I'm Serenity Chandler. I have an appointment with Tammy to finalize some paperwork before starting Monday."

"Oh! Of course." She shuffled some papers around in front of her. "My name's Maggie. I think we're going to be working together. Which is great, we've been shorthanded up front for a while." She turned her attention to Gideon. "And who do we have here?"

"This is my son, Gideon. He'll be attending the school starting Monday as well. Kindergarten, right buddy?" Serenity put an arm around his shoulders and patted his chest. "When I spoke with Tammy on the phone, she said one of his new teachers would take him to the gym while I got things settled."

Maggie gave him a wave "It's nice to meet you, Gideon. Welcome to Hope Academy. I think you're going to like it here." She picked up a phone. "Let me call for Letty. I have a note saying she'll be Gideon's teacher. She's here and I'm sure she'd be happy for the chance to get to know him a little. I'll inform Tammy as well."

Serenity nodded. "I appreciate that." Good. Letty was the one who evaluated Gideon when they came a few weeks ago. She would be familiar and hopefully he wouldn't mind going with her.

They chatted for a few minutes until Letty arrived. As soon as she saw Gideon, she knelt down to his level and waved. "It's great to see you again, Gideon! Would you like to come and play for a while? We're going to have a lot of fun." His experience during his evaluation must have been a good one because he immediately took a step towards her.

Serenity ruffled his hair. "Make sure you mind Miss Letty. I'll see you in a little while."

Letty took his hand. "We'll be fine. Take as long as you need to." She turned to Maggie. "Call when you're ready and I'll bring him back up here."

Serenity watched them disappear from sight, comforted by the fact that he never even hesitated. She'd been praying that the school would be the perfect fit for him. For both of them. Moving away from home was huge and she needed this to work.

A door opened on the other side of the room and Tammy walked in. "Hi, Serenity. It's good to see you again. Are you getting settled in your new place?"

"We are, thank you. It'll take some time, but we like the neighborhood pretty well so far."

"Great to hear. If you'll come back to my office, we'll finish up some paperwork and then I'll let Maggie introduce you to some of what you'll be doing Monday morning."

By the time Serenity rejoined Maggie out front, she'd lost count of how many times she'd signed her name.

Maggie explained to her how to check parents in if they were going into the school and how to scan the printed stickers to show they'd left. "It's part of the security system and we do it to keep the kids safe. We want the parents to be able to go back with the kids or participate, but we can't let just anyone walk in off the streets."

"I agree completely." Serenity tapped the plastic badge she'd clipped to the hem of her shirt. "It'll be nice to have the ID."

A deep voice brought their attention away from the

computer. "Hey, Maggie. Has FedEx dropped anything off yet this morning?"

Serenity's gaze followed the voice and found a man striding towards the desk with a stack of papers in his large hands. Dark auburn hair curled slightly where it touched the tops of his ears and the base of his neck. He carried himself with purpose, his clean-shaven jaw working as he leafed through the papers.

"They haven't been by yet. If anything comes in for you, I'll give you a shout." Maggie shot him a wink, even though he hadn't raised his head yet to catch it.

"That'll be great, thanks."

He moved away from them and Serenity didn't think he was even going to look up. But his eyes lifted at the last moment, going first to Maggie with a hint of wariness and then landing on her. His dark blue eyes widened slightly and the hand that still held the papers lowered.

Serenity shifted in her seat. How one pair of eyes could make her feel self-aware and curious about him at the same time, she had no idea.

Maggie chuckled. "I take it you two haven't met yet. Aaron Randall, this is my new desk buddy, Serenity Chandler. She'll be starting on Monday, I'm showing her the ropes for a couple of hours this morning. Serenity, Aaron is our music therapist. He's been with the school for several years now and is one of our most eligible bachelors."

~

Anxious to get the shipment of rainbow hand bells Aaron had ordered, he thought he'd check and see if it'd arrived. Before entering the room, he steeled himself against Maggie. He was confident the woman would flirt with an unattached orangutan if given the chance. He made a point of not being alone with her in a room if he could help it. Even after she told him FedEx hadn't been by yet, he could have sworn he felt her wink.

Aaron didn't like to be rude, even when she made him uncomfortable. He was glancing up to give Maggie a nod of thanks. That's when he saw *her*.

Serenity was such a contrast to the woman training her. Maggie wore copious amounts of makeup and her hair color changed every other week — he seriously doubted even she knew what color her hair was before the first bottle of dye.

On the other hand, Serenity's rich brown hair was so dark it was nearly black. It flowed like a waterfall down her back, making him wonder how long it really was. If she was wearing any makeup, he couldn't tell.

He stepped forward and extended a hand. "It's nice to meet you." She placed a much smaller hand in his, her touch sending a jolt of awareness from there straight to his heart. He cleared his throat in an attempt to hide his reaction. "Welcome to Hope Academy. You'll enjoy working here — for the most part. Just watch out for this one." He jerked his head towards Maggie, who only laughed in response. "She thinks any single guy is eligible."

Maggie threw her head back and laughed loudly, her red curls bobbing with her giggles. "You bet I do."

Serenity smiled. "That's good to know." She hesitated. "It's going to take a while to get the hang of everything. But so far, everyone's been very welcoming."

Aaron couldn't look away from her brown eyes

framed just right with long, dark eyelashes. There was a small, circular scar at the corner of her right eye and he wondered how she'd gotten it.

Forcing himself to break eye contact, he cleared his throat again and released her hand, immediately missing the connection. "I wish you the best of luck Monday, then."

"I appreciate that." Serenity's smile was hesitant and didn't quite reach her eyes.

Aaron made a hasty retreat, but he wasn't quick enough. Maggie's voice could be heard behind him, "What'd I tell you? Dreamy, right? I'd like to be the one to take him off the market."

He groaned and rolled his eyes. With a total of only three unattached men working at the school, he didn't have a lot of hope that Maggie would set her sights on someone else. He was used to being employed in an environment where he was vastly outnumbered by women — until he was in the same room as Maggie.

With other things to do, he forced all thoughts of Maggie from his head. As his footsteps echoed down the hallway, he realized it wouldn't be as easy to do the same with Serenity.

Especially when all he could see were those eyes that reminded him of warm, melted chocolate.

Chapter Four

Milk sloshed out of the bowl when Serenity poured it, leaving a puddle on the table. Gideon wasted no time in sticking his tongue out to lick it. She snatched a rag off the counter, mopped up the mess, and handed him a spoon for good measure.

"I promise, Mom. We're fine." She moved her cell phone from one ear to the other. "We're all set to start work and school on Monday. Gideon's been to the school twice now. They gave me his schedule and we've gone over it several times. We're both about as ready as we can be."

Serenity wanted to be annoyed that Mom had called every single morning since she and Gideon moved out. But the truth was, having never lived on her own, she dearly missed the sound of both Mom's and Grams' voices. Besides, the Chandler house would be getting ready for church and then, later that evening, meeting for family dinner.

She couldn't remember the last time she'd missed one. The thought brought tears to her eyes. She furiously blinked them away. Mom would catch on if there was even a hint of sadness in her voice and the last thing she wanted was for Mom to worry.

"How about the people you work with? Are they nice?"

Serenity was glad for the distraction. Although the shift in thoughts brought a new one in the form of a handsome man with auburn hair and unforgettable blue eyes. Keeping him out of the conversation, she told Mom about Maggie in great detail. They both had a good laugh. Serenity suspected that beneath Maggie's tough – and obnoxious — exterior was someone who enjoyed being around people and was probably good at her job.

"I miss you, honey. But I hope you know I'm proud of you, too."

What control she'd gained over her tears disappeared. One escaped to slide down her cheek. "I miss you, too, Mom. Look, I'd better let you go so you can get ready for church."

"Okay. Once you get settled, you'll have to ask around and find a church there."

"I will."

"Have a good morning. Call me tomorrow evening and let me know how your first day goes."

"Promise. Love you, Mom. Give everyone else my love, too." Serenity set her phone on the counter and kissed the top of Gideon's head.

She had every intention of finding a new church, although the idea itself seemed overwhelming. Maybe she would meet some people at the school and could ask which churches they attended.

Aaron's face came to mind and she mentally shrugged it off. Like she had the other two dozen times she'd thought about him since first meeting him the other day.

A scuffling noise brought her head around to face the door. She half expected someone to knock. When there were no other sounds, she peeped through the hole in the door and didn't see a thing.

Maybe having a cop for an older brother made her overly cautious, but she decided not to open it. It wasn't until later when she and Gideon were headed to the store for a few last minute items that she saw a navy blue backpack resting against the side of their duplex.

Serenity cast a suspicious glimpse up and down the street before nudging it with her foot. A sign pinned to the front pocket read, "For your first day of school, Gideon. Welcome to Hope Academy."

She grasped it by the loop on top, surprised by how heavy it was. Gideon followed her to the kitchen table. As soon as she sat it down, he went to task unzipping the pockets and pulling everything out.

"This is insanely generous," she muttered, taking inventory.

Every school item a boy might need in kindergarten was accounted for, from safety scissors to a superhero notebook. On top of that, there were all kinds of snacks.

No one at Hope Academy had mentioned a thing about a welcoming package. It was certainly more than she ever would have expected. She'd have to make a point of thanking someone tomorrow.

~

Aaron grinned as he held the door open to his music room and watched Letty's kindergarten class come through. Their little faces lit up as they took in their surroundings. For many of them, this was their first trip there. Only those who had started coming to Hope Academy as preschoolers were familiar with the layout. Letty brought up the rear and closed the door behind her.

He smiled at her. "How's your first day going?"

"It's going well! A bit like herding cats, but that's to be expected for the first week or two with a new class." She chuckled. "I think the rug's a hit."

Aaron followed her gaze. Cecil, who had been coming to the school since he was four, spotted the piano rug immediately. He'd stretched out on the floor, his body angled the same direction as the first key, a look of pure joy lighting up his face. Methodically, he rolled his body across each of them, humming a tone as he did. "Those notes are right on."

"The boy knows his music." Letty's love for her students was evident to anyone who met her.

Aaron couldn't agree more. While some people might meet Cecil and see a child with Down syndrome, Aaron saw a little boy with sandy brown hair who had a kind heart, a gentle spirit, and who would likely become a musician someday.

Most of the kids had found an instrument in the bins to play with. The conglomerate of random sounds and notes filled the room. There were a lot of new little faces.

One boy in particular drew his attention. He had dark brown hair that was nearly black. His arms carried an entire bin full of the hand bells Aaron had finally received and found himself a spot on the edge of the room. One by one, he pulled them out and lined them up in order of color according to the rainbow. Aaron angled his head in the boy's direction.

"Autism?"

Letty nodded. "That's Gideon. He'll be six in a few months. He just started today. He's non-verbal, but knows some signs and gestures. I got to spend a few hours with him on Friday. He was friendly and relaxed then but I think all of the kids are a little overwhelming today."

Aaron picked up a small, red bell that he kept on his desk and rang it loudly. That gained the attention of all eight children in the room. "Hi, everyone! My name is Aaron and I'm glad you're here. Do you know what everyone calls me? I'm the Music Man!" He picked up a guitar and strummed a few chords. "Every time you come to my room, you'll get to play with anything you see for ten minutes." He reached for the visual timer he used and set it. "When this timer goes off, we're going to sit in a circle so we can talk about some music, then we'll learn about an instrument, and sing a few songs. How does that sound?"

Happy faces and a few shouts of "Yay!" followed his question. Two little girls seemed uncertain about it and Gideon continued to keep his focus on the hand bells.

That was okay. Each year, it took a week or two to get the kids into the routine. Before long, they would all know what was expected and things would go relatively smoothly. There was always going to be a kink or two, but that's what kept things interesting. He smiled to himself.

He crossed the room and sat next to Gideon. There was something about the boy that reminded him of his little brother, Kenneth. The realization was painful but there was also a strange peace in it as well. He missed

Kenneth even after almost two decades and sitting next to Gideon soothed that little piece of his heart.

Now that the boy had the bells in order by color, he was picking them up and studying the note etched into the side of each one.

"Those are musical notes." Aaron pointed to one of them. "That's a C. This is a B." When he picked up the orange bell, Gideon retrieved it from him and set it quickly back in its place in line. "Have you tried making music with them yet?" Gideon said nothing but he didn't seem to object, so Aaron picked up the red bell, rang it, and set it down in its place. "That's an A note. Why don't you ring the next one?"

Gideon did as he suggested and continued on down the line until the last bell had filled the room with its tone. When it faded, Gideon peeked up at Aaron with a smile on his face that lit up his eyes. There was something about him that seemed familiar, not only because he reminded him of Kenneth, but he couldn't quite put his finger on why.

"Good job, kiddo. Maybe one of these days I can teach you how to play a song with the bells. Would you like that?"

The timer went off then. He and Letty worked together to place carpet squares in a circle and led the children to their spots. Then they sat down among them, Letty supporting one of the younger children who had trouble sitting upright.

Aaron let his gaze touch each of their faces, saying a quick prayer that he would be able to make a difference in their young lives. If there was one thing he learned in his years at Hope Academy, it was that no matter what type of challenge each of the children faced — and whether it was evident on the outside or hidden within — every single one was a gift from God and he was humbled to have a part in teaching them.

He smiled at them. "Who can tell me the name of an instrument?"

"Guitar!"

"Drums!"

"Piano!"

It was no surprise that the last one came from Cecil. Aaron chuckled. "That's right. Anyone else? What other instruments can you think of?" He watched Gideon as the boy's eyes went from him to the bin of hand bells and back again. "That's right, Gideon. Bells are a kind of instrument, too. Did you know that your voices can be an instrument as well? Each instrument plays a part in making music."

He got his guitar and played "Twinkle, Twinkle Little Star," inviting the kids to sing if they knew the song. The combination of little voices made his own heart sing. And even though Gideon didn't say a word, he seemed to enjoy the antics of his classmates around him.

Aaron had fun teaching Letty's class and later had individual music therapy sessions with two other students. By the time lunch came around, his stomach was growling.

He headed for the breakroom, more than ready to dig into the cold pizza he'd stashed in the community fridge. His stomach growled in anticipation. He didn't expect to see too many other people in the kitchen since it was nearly one and that was fine by him.

As soon as he entered, his eyes zeroed in on the woman he'd met at the front office the other day. She was holding a book in one hand, a sandwich in the other, and seemed completely oblivious to him or anyone else in the room.

Aaron retrieved his pizza from the fridge and got a soda from the vending machine. He started to head to his usual table in the corner but there was something about her that stopped him. He sure hated to leave her there eating alone on her first day of work.

Changing direction, he approached her. She kept her attention on the book until he cleared his throat. Her head lifted and her gaze snapped to his.

"I'm sorry. I didn't see you." Her cheeks took on a slight hint of pink. She allowed the book to close and set it down on the table. "I met you last week. Aaron, right?"

"Good memory. And you're Serenity." He glanced at her left hand, noting the lack of a wedding ring.

She smiled. "Your memory's not bad, either."

In a lunch room filled with way too many food smells, the light scent of lilac surrounding her was a welcome change. He latched onto it, finding himself drawn to the pretty woman sitting in front of him.

Chapter Five

Serenity wondered if Aaron was trying to decide whether or not he wanted to stay. His blue eyes were on her and she could have sworn the edges had darkened to cobalt. He blinked and motioned to the table.

"Well, it's good to see you again. Do you mind if I join you?"

"Not at all. I guess I'm not the only one who gets a late lunch."

Aaron sat across from her and started peeling the layers of aluminum foil off his plate. "I arrange lunch for this time. It gets pretty crowded in here if you come around noon. Especially if you need to use the microwave."

"Is there a lunch thief on campus?" Confusion flitted across his face and she chuckled. She pointed to the aluminum foil and the numerous times he'd written his name on it.

"Oh." He laughed. "Only once. It was actually Zane — one of my friends here. I stole his lunch the next day. Now it's tradition for us to write our names all over our lunches. It's just for fun, of course." He looked at her in mock seriousness. "Unless I bring leftover Mexican food. Then I have to hide it in the back somewhere so Zane doesn't touch it."

He laughed again and Serenity found the deep tone worked its way right to the center of her. There was something about it that made her comfortable, though she couldn't explain it. "I'll have to remember that. You going to eat it cold?"

"The pizza? Yep." He took an exaggerated bite. "It's the only way to eat leftover pizza."

With a grin, she took a bite of her sandwich. Since it contained packaged chicken lunch meat and a swipe of honey mustard on the bread, she had to admit that his pizza smelled a whole lot tastier. "Do I remember right that you're a music therapist? What does that mean, exactly?"

Aaron put his pizza down and his face lit up. "I spend half my time as a glorified music teacher. The other half, I work one-on-one with kids who are referred to me by their teachers. I've seen music help kids talk more. I even had one little boy with a lot of self-injurious behavior improve once we realized how much classical music relaxed him. He has an iPod with him now and when he starts to get frustrated or upset, he knows to put in the earbuds and listen to his favorite song."

"Really? That's amazing." She was fascinated as much by his excitement as she was by his words. "What made you decide to go into this line of work?"

Aaron shrugged and picked up his pizza again. "It's a long story." He took a bite and chewed it thoughtfully. "But I can't imagine doing anything else."

A pang of jealousy hit her in the chest. Sometimes she wished she could be as enthusiastic about something in her own life. Aside from Gideon, that is. For all of her adulthood, everything revolved around trying to provide for her son. The jobs she'd had were a means to an end and certainly not something she truly loved.

Thankfully, Aaron didn't seem to notice the mess of thoughts going through her head. He took a drink of his lemon lime soda.

"Are you doing okay working with Maggie?"

Thinking about her co-worker elicited a chuckle. "She's actually been incredibly helpful. I've worked a similar job in the past and it's already been more exciting here on the first day."

Aaron finished his pizza and crumpled the aluminum foil. "It is a great place to work." He checked his watch. "I've got another class coming in so I'd better run." He stood and paused. "I hope the rest of your day goes well. Maybe I'll see you tomorrow?"

Now that he was standing again, he seemed to tower over her. She also got the sense that he was older than she was, though she wasn't sure by how much. She managed a friendly nod.

The way he winked one of his blue eyes and the sound of his deep laughter stayed with her the rest of the day. If eating lunch together became a frequent thing, she had a feeling it would be her favorite part of the workday. Nerves collided with anticipation at the thought as she worked to finish her sandwich and get back to the front office.

~

"I hear you've been having lunch with the new lady in administration all week."

Aaron pierced Zane with a "don't start with me" glare and put the last of the disinfected instruments away. "We happen to have lunch at the same time and there's usually only a few of us there after one. It would have been rude to ignore her and leave her by herself."

Zane lifted an eyebrow and Aaron pretended to ignore it. "But you find her attractive."

Aaron cast a glance at the door to make sure no one else was around. "I'd be lying if I said she wasn't. But it's a general observation."

"Of course." He waited for Aaron to finish up then led the way out of the room and down the hall. "Hey, you up for going to see that new movie this weekend?"

As if Aaron ever turned down a Marvel movie. "Absolutely. Is Letty going?"

Zane chuckled. "Of course. Superheroes and Red Vines. She wouldn't miss it."

"You sure I won't be a third wheel?"

"Invite your lunch friend and then you won't be." Zane nudged him hard in the ribs.

"Very funny." Truthfully, he didn't mind being the third in their group. It happened often and his married friends never made him uncomfortable. But Zane's lighthearted suggestion got him thinking about asking Serenity to go along. Which was crazy because eating lunch with her at work was a long ways from asking her out. "I wouldn't dare risk the wrath of Cynthia."

Zane's face contorted into a look of disdain. "Who would? But for the record, the memo said you couldn't date a student's mother. It never said you couldn't show interest in someone else working here."

Technically, that was true. A little hope welled up in his chest. Maybe, at some point in the future, it wouldn't be such a stretch to ask her to go to a movie with him.

"Where are you guys headed?" Letty's voice floated up the hall behind them. They stopped and waited for her to catch up.

Zane put an arm around her shoulders and drew her close. "I was about to come find you. Right after I convinced Music Man here to bring a date to the movies with us this weekend."

Letty's eyes widened and a smile tugged the corners of her lips upwards. "You should, Aaron. It'd be good for you. Who's the lucky gal?"

Aaron cast a glance behind them and lowered his voice. "Your husband thinks I should ask the new woman in administration."

"They've already had lunch together." Zane chuckled.

Aaron was about to object and then decided not to bother. Zane could tease ruthlessly when he got on a roll. It was better not to encourage it either way.

"Serenity?"

Aaron nodded, curious to see what Letty thought about the idea, and said, "She seems nice enough. Although I think Zane might be jumping the gun a little, here."

Letty frowned. "Aren't you worried about Cynthia's new guidelines?"

Aaron exchanged an equally confused look with Zane. "I think they're insane. But what does that have to do with Serenity?"

Letty's eyes widened. "Didn't you know? She's got a son going to Hope. You met him on Monday.

Remember Gideon?"

The little boy immediately came to mind. He remembered vaguely thinking he seemed familiar. Now he realized why: Both mother and son had the same chocolate-colored eyes.

He blew out a puff of air and shrugged. "I remember him. I hadn't made the connection. So much for your matchmaking skills, Zane." Aaron was trying to be nonchalant. It wasn't easy when the idea of asking Serenity out had seemed like such a good one at the time.

He was certainly glad Letty made the connection between Serenity and Gideon, though. With her in administration, Aaron likely wouldn't see her often anyway. It was probably just as well. Dating wasn't something he usually made time for, and when he did, he couldn't seem to connect with the women on a personal level. Serenity being the mother of one of his students was an additional layer of complication he didn't need in his life. The last thing he wanted was Cynthia breathing down his neck.

Aaron bid his friends farewell and headed towards the parking lot. He considered eating at his desk in his classroom instead of the breakroom so that he wouldn't risk spending too much time with Serenity.

But as soon as the thought entered his mind, he dismissed it. He wasn't going to run away. He barely knew the woman. All he had to do was keep treating her like he did any of his other co-workers. He could be friends with the new lady in administration.

The new beautiful lady who smelled like lavender and had one of the prettiest smiles he'd ever seen.

Yep, it ought to be easy.

Chapter Six

Serenity managed to survive her first week at Hope Academy and felt like it was relatively successful. While she had a lot to learn, at least she wasn't stumbling over the computer keys when checking visitors in. And she knew how to replace the roll of adhesive name tags that printed out as temporary badges.

Gideon seemed to have a good first week as well. She heard mostly encouraging reports from Letty and the notes she'd received from his speech and occupational therapists were all positive as well. By the end of the week, they'd started to settle into their new routine. Letty kept Gideon after school ended for an extra half hour in the classroom. When Serenity got off work at four in the afternoon, she picked him up and they headed home.

Their second weekend in the Dallas area was a strangely relaxing one. The idea of having spare time was nearly foreign to Serenity. When she was employed at the restaurant, extra hours were worked in whenever she could get them. They were living pay check to pay check now, and while she felt tempted to find work on the weekends, for the first time in her life she had no one to keep Gideon. And she wasn't about to find a random day care for him.

Besides, Lexi had made her promise to give it six months in their current situation before trying to locate any other type of work. She was the only one Serenity had confided in when it came to her financial situation. Both of them were shocked and thrilled when Serenity had not only gotten the job at Hope Academy, but Gideon had received such a large scholarship. One that size was virtually unheard of.

"It's a God thing," Lexi had told her. "Which means you need to give Him a chance to work the rest of it out. Don't try to push it."

Serenity knew she was right. Even if Gideon didn't receive the scholarship again next year, he would have one year at an amazing school. She had to focus on that.

After doing a lot of reading over the weekend and checking out the local parks, she and Gideon both felt ready to tackle a new week.

When she dropped him off at his classroom, Letty stopped her before she left. "Will you have about twenty minutes after you get off work? I wanted to talk to you about getting Gideon into some one-on-one music therapy. I think it would benefit him."

"Oh, sure. That'll be fine." Serenity tried to imagine what all would take place during the session and was grateful she would have the chance to ask her questions.

"Great! Meet me here like usual and we'll walk over to the music room. Aaron will wait for us there."

Serenity nodded her understanding, gave Gideon a

kiss goodbye, and made her way through the maze of hallways back to the front of the school.

All the while, Aaron remained on her mind. They'd eaten lunch together almost every day. Sometimes someone else joined them, and other times it was just the two of them. Either way, she always enjoyed the company. They usually kept conversation light and centered on activities within the school. Aaron rarely asked her any personal questions and she'd taken her cue from him.

The day quickly turned into a typical Monday. Two kiddos came into the office sick, keeping the nurse, Candace, on her toes. The printer jammed, a parent came in and yelled at them for losing a permission slip, and Serenity spilled her water. Thankfully, she'd managed to mop up the mess before it soaked through the papers on her desk.

Halfway into the morning, Aaron came through the office, giving her a nod and a small smile on his way out.

Maggie grinned at Serenity. "I think he may be interested in you."

"I seriously doubt that." The suggestion alone caused heat to flood her cheeks. "We don't even know anything about each other."

"The Music Man is a busy guy. But I'd be willing to bet he's come through the office about three times as often since you started working than he did before." Maggie winked, her blue eyeshadow the same shade as the streaks in her hair. "I'm pretty sure it's not because he's got a sudden interest in yours truly."

Serenity shot her a dubious look and focused on the flyers she was stuffing into envelopes. On the inside, her mind was running ninety miles an hour, trying to process what her co-worker had just said. There was no way Aaron had an interest in her.

Besides, the moment a guy found out she was a single mom with a child who had autism, any interest that did exist dissipated. It'd happened to her a couple of times and she'd reached a place in her life where she was okay with that. Or, at least, that's what she told herself regularly. Most of the time the pep talk worked.

By the time four o'clock came around, Serenity's thoughts had worked her stomach into a knot. Picking at a hangnail, she made her way to Letty's classroom. Gideon glanced up from his spot by the blocks and grinned.

That smile — those sparkling eyes — it made everything worth it. The tension she'd been carrying across her shoulders all day melted away. She sat on the floor with him, pulling him into a hug. "How'd your day go, big guy? Did you build that tower?"

Gideon patted the top block that was a little taller than him. A mischievous look passed over his face and the next moment, he executed a fantastic roundhouse kick, knocking the blocks into a heap on the floor.

Letty joined them as she laughed. "Good job, Gideon. All right, let's clean up and then go visit the Music Man."

As soon as he heard that, he rushed to stack the blocks in a series of piles near the wall. When he finished, he grabbed Serenity's hand and tried to drag her through the door and out into the hallway.

Apparently her son liked visiting the Music Man. It made her even more curious to see what his classroom was like.

As they walked down the halls, Letty asked, "How do you guys like the area? Do you attend a church?"

"Our neighborhood seems nice. We live in a duplex, but I have no complaints about the man who lives next door. And no, we haven't found a church. I've gone to the same one since I was a child, so I admit I'm overwhelmed by the prospect."

"I completely understand. You're welcome to visit ours. Zane and I go to a friendly one a few blocks from here. It's the only church in town that has a dedicated children's class for special needs. I've heard nothing but good things about it."

Serenity had to admit that sounded tempting. She asked her several questions about the church as they neared their destination and finally agreed to go with Letty and Zane the next Sunday.

There was no missing the music classroom. Entering it was like walking right into a colorful world all of its own. No wonder Gideon couldn't wait to go back.

She took in the colorful rug and posters on the wall, bins of instruments, and the line of music that ran from one wall to the other.

Her focus went to the man seated at his desk. When he saw them, he stood and walked towards him. How was it that, in a room full of color, his blue eyes seemed to outshine everything else?

~

Aaron tried to stay busy all afternoon, looking forward to the meeting with Serenity. When the trio walked in, he welcomed them with a wave. He knelt down and held out a hand towards Gideon, face up. "It's good to see you, kiddo. Can I have a five?" The boy obliged, his eyes darting around the room. "I'll bet

I know what you'd like to play with." Gideon's eyes focused on him, filled with expectations and questions. "Are you kidding? Go get 'em!"

He ran straight to the bin of hand bells and pulled it over to the carpet.

Serenity watched him take out one bell after another. "Now I know why he was excited to come back here."

She chuckled and Aaron drank in the sound of it. He'd been held up at lunch and didn't see her. He didn't think it would make a difference until he'd gone through the whole weekend and then today without talking to her. Apparently their friendly lunches were becoming addicting.

He caught Letty watching him, her brows drawn together in concern. He hoped the barely perceptible shake of his head put her at ease.

With a deep breath, Aaron took on his teacher role and tried to bury everything else plaguing his mind. "Gideon's a great kid. Letty brings his class by on Mondays for music. You can probably guess what instrument is his favorite."

Serenity bobbed her head. "I could certainly speculate. I'm surprised you get him to leave again."

Letty laughed. "It's not easy. All of the kids love coming to see the Music Man." She tilted her head towards Aaron. "I don't know if he told you or not, but Aaron also does a lot of one-on-one music therapy with some of the kids. We've been talking and we think Gideon would benefit from it."

Serenity smiled at Gideon. "It's definitely something I'm interested in for him. What exactly does a music therapy session contain? What are your goals?"

They were good questions. Serenity's pretty brown

eyes were on him, waiting for his response.

"I usually start out with a song. In Gideon's case, since he's non-verbal, we'll be singing songs that have a lot of hand motions or dancing to them. That way I can get him moving and give him motivation to try and copy what I'm doing." Aaron found that mimicking was something a lot of kids with autism struggled with and, so far, he'd seen the same with Gideon. "After that, we'll work on a particular task. Whether that's learning to play an instrument or studying a music note. Finally, we'll have a question and answer session and then that'll be it. It will last twenty to thirty minutes, depending on how he's doing that day."

He watched Gideon leave the hand bells lined up and start to explore another bin. "It may take us a week or two to get our footing. But the ultimate goal is to help him initiate interactions, extend his attention span, and use music to help with alternative communication skills. I'm looking forward to working with him."

Aaron never tired of seeing kids connect with him and others through music in a way they were unable to otherwise. It was a true gift from God to be able to be a part of it.

Serenity seemed happy with his responses. "I think he'll like that. Any extra therapy he can get is a good thing." She hesitated, almost as if she were trying to get the courage to speak. "I was nervous about moving here like we did. We left a lot behind to come to this school. It's only been a week and it's exceeded my expectations. Thank you both."

Moisture gathered in her eyes, reminding him of molten chocolate. She sniffed quietly and Letty put an arm around her shoulders, hugging her. "Sometimes it's almost overwhelming when we see evidence that

God's taking care of us, isn't it?"

Serenity nodded and leaned into Letty, swiping at the corners of her eyes.

Something told Aaron that Serenity had been through a lot and she wasn't the type to reveal much about herself. He was probably a glutton for punishment because right then, he wished he were the one offering her a hug.

He'd made a point of keeping their conversations basic and somewhat impersonal in hopes of not fueling the attraction he felt towards her. If the pulse in his ears and the ache in his heart were any indication, it wasn't working.

Chapter Seven

Zane and Letty insisted on picking up Serenity and Gideon at their house so they could go to church with them. Serenity had tried to object, more than once throughout the week, but they wouldn't hear of it. She finally relented. Zane moved Gideon's booster seat over and they were soon on their way.

During the drive, she discovered the church was situated about halfway between her house and the school. It was insane how everything was so close together. What were the odds? On a nice day, she and Gideon could easily walk to the church.

Serenity couldn't remember not attending her family's church. Hands shaking, she smoothed down the loose-fitting blouse for the third time since they'd left the house. Walking up to the large, brick building turned the butterflies in her stomach to airplanes.

She shouldn't have worried. From the moment they stepped through those front doors, she and Gideon were greeted with smiles and handshakes. Zane and

Letty introduced them to several people they knew and then helped them find the correct classroom for Gideon.

The class setup for special needs kids contained everything from building blocks to a tent filled with cushions. Gideon ran right in, dove into the cushions, and rewarded Serenity with a grin.

Serenity visited with his Sunday school teachers, telling them a little about her son and filling out some information. She was given a number that was assigned to him and told that if they needed anything, his number would appear on the screen in the worship hall.

Gideon seemed more than happy to stay, but Serenity still hesitated to leave him. Letty appeared out of nowhere beside her. "He's in good hands. I've known Aster for years. She used to work at Hope so she knows what she's doing."

That made Serenity feel a little better. She and Letty caught up with Zane in the worship hall. He was waiting for them in one of the back rows. Serenity claimed her seat and perused the bulletin she'd been handed on the way in.

The worship leader opened the morning with prayer. When he'd finished, the lights came on over the stage revealing six members of the worship team. Serenity's eyes immediately went to the man in the back left. She leaned closer to Letty. "Is that Aaron?"

Letty nodded. "He's played keyboard for the worship team for several years now. He's really good."

Serenity watched as his fingers touched the keys, his eyes closed as he sang along with everyone else. The songs were heartfelt, leading to a sense of peace and closeness to God. It'd only been three weeks, but she'd missed this. When Aaron stepped forward to lead one chorus, Serenity was completely unprepared for how deep his voice was. His speaking voice was lower than average, but nothing like this. Chill bumps sprang up along her arms as the bass filled the room.

His was the kind of tone that would sell a lot of CDs if he ever chose to record. Yet, he was working at a special needs school and playing music for his church.

Aaron Randall was one surprise after another.

~

After worship, Aaron made his way to the back of the church to join his friends. The last thing he expected, when he gained his seat next to Zane, was to see Serenity two chairs down. "Good morning," he greeted her, his mind going in all different directions. He leaned over and whispered to Zane, "You could have warned me."

Zane smirked at him. "According to what you've told me, I didn't think it mattered."

Aaron pretended like he didn't hear his friend. He leaned down to retrieve his Bible from beneath his seat, giving him an opportunity for a quick glance at Serenity. She'd pulled part of her hair into a clasp at the back of her head. Shorter strands fell along her jaw and his fingers itched to tuck them behind her ears. It was a fight to direct his thoughts back to the church service, and it proved to be only partially successful.

After the final prayer, everyone stood to gather their things. Letty turned to Serenity.

"We planned to go to out for brunch after church today. You and Gideon are welcome to join us. It's our treat."

The invitation had barely been uttered and Serenity was shaking her head. "We don't want to impose."

"You're not imposing." Zane gave his wife a peck on the cheek. "You'll be doing Letty a favor, adding a little more estrogen to the mix."

Serenity's cheeks turned a pretty shade of pink and Aaron's heart rate increased when she nodded.

"We appreciate it, thank you."

By the time they all caravanned from the church to the restaurant, Aaron was more than ready for lunch. They had to wait for a table, but once they got seated, their waitress took the orders quickly. Gideon stayed busy doing a dot-to-dot on the back of the kid's menu with the crayons he'd been given.

Aaron was conscious of Serenity sitting in the chair next to his. She and Letty were talking about Hope Academy. He was half listening, since Zane was talking about baseball scores at the same time.

It wasn't until Serenity mentioned something about the school giving Gideon a backpack that his full attention was jerked towards her. "What was that?"

Her brows drew together. "Last Sunday, we found a backpack leaning against our front porch. It had a ton of school supplies in it along with snacks. Someone put a sign on it saying it was from Hope Academy." Her eyes narrowed. "Was it not?"

Aaron shared a look with Zane. "As far as I know, the school's never done that. Even if they did, I think they'd have given it to you during the introductory tour. I doubt they would have dropped it off at your house." Serenity seemed nervous and he rushed to put her at ease. "I didn't mean to worry you. It's probably something new they're trying this year." Or maybe one of her family members left it there to surprise them?

Serenity nodded. "That makes sense. It was certainly a big help and Gideon will use everything they put in the backpack."

The bright smile she offered him was completely captivating. He spent the rest of their time together finding ways to make that smile appear again.

~

Several days later, Aaron stepped out of the air conditioned school and into the humid warmth. He stopped and squinted at the late August sky. A wall of dark clouds approached from the distance. That, in addition to the unusually heavy feel to the air, suggested thunderstorms were on their way.

Ready to go home and relax for the rest of the afternoon and evening, he headed for his black Volkswagen at the back of the parking lot. Movement snagged his attention. He zeroed in on a pair of legs sticking out from beneath an older Kia, the engine running. Almost certain he knew who those legs belonged to, he knelt down on one knee and lowered his head to the pavement.

"Serenity? What are you doing?"

She scrambled out from under the car and stood up quickly. Brushing her hands off on her pants only added to the dirt smudges already there. "Shhhh! Listen."

Aaron spotted Gideon sitting in the back seat of the car and thought maybe she was referring to him. A moment later, the faintest meow reached his ears. "A cat?"

Serenity nodded quickly. "I think it's a kitten. It's stuck up under my car. I can't drive home knowing it's under there. What if that kills it?" Her eyes brimmed with concern and her voice shook. "I was trying to reach it so I could pull it out."

There were several strays in the area. One of them must have had a litter of kittens and one had crawled up under the car to get out of the sun earlier that day. It was the only explanation he could think of. "Can you actually see it when you're under there?"

"Yep, right over the rear tire."

She was watching him, her face full of hope, the storm clouds reflected in her eyes. How could he not offer to help? He set his messenger bag on the ground. "Let me give it a try."

"Are you sure? I don't want you to get filthy. I'm hoping I'll be able to coax it out."

He held back a chuckle, imagining her under there calling, "Here, kitty, kitty," and waiting for the feline to jump down on its own. If the increasing volume of the meows was any indication, it wasn't likely to come out willingly. And he wasn't about to leave her out here in the parking lot with the storm rolling in.

Gideon opened a car door and jumped out. He ran around the back and joined his mom. She put a hand on his shoulder. "The Music Man is going to try to get the kitty out from under the car and then we can go home." The boy looked at him expectantly.

Show time.

He eased himself under the edge of the car. The cat's cry for help was much louder and he quickly saw two reflecting eyes staring back at him. As long as the cat didn't try to wedge itself in any further, Aaron was sure he could pull it out. Avoiding claws might be a different story.

"It's okay, we're going to get you out of here. And

let's try to remember never to climb up under a car again, huh?" He kept his voice soothing as he reached for the cat, his hand closing on the scruff of its neck. A panicked mew along with an attempt to scramble away from him resulted but he kept a firm hold as he eased the cat out of the space it'd crawled into.

Aaron felt the sharp pebbles in the pavement against his back as he moved out from beneath the car and stood. They got the first real view of the small animal in his hands.

A pair of blue eyes stared at the three of them, wide and uncertain.

Serenity reached for the cat and he transferred it to her. "Poor little thing. I think it's Siamese."

"At least partly." There was no mistaking the coloring of the fur in combination with those eyes. He couldn't recall seeing a stray Siamese, but then it could have wandered from almost anywhere.

She tipped the animal slightly before bringing it to her chest with both hands. "She's a girl." It wasn't long before her breathing slowed and she relaxed.

Gideon reached up and touched her softly. He ran a hand over the cat's head and she closed her eyes. He patted his chest and reached his arms out.

"Oh, big guy, I don't know. She might run off." Gideon patted his chest again. Serenity relented. "Okay, but hold her close to you so she feels safe."

Aaron watched as the boy took the animal in his arms in a much gentler way than he'd expected. The kitten rubbed her little head against the bottom of Gideon's chin and started to purr. Aaron's little brother had liked cats, too, even though their parents had refused to get one. Though Kenneth hadn't been quite as gentle with them as Gideon was now.

Serenity seemed stunned. "He's always liked my brother's dog, but never got attached to him. He seems to like this kitten, though."

"The feeling appears to be mutual." He brushed some dirt off the back of his arm. "What are you going to do?"

"How can I not take her home now?" She put a hand on her son's shoulder. "What do you think, Gideon? Should we take her home and she can be our cat?"

He turned, held the cat with one hand, and pulled the car door open with the other.

Serenity chuckled. "Gideon. Look at me. Does that mean yes? You need to tell me." He nodded once and climbed into the vehicle. "There we have it." She turned her attention to Aaron. "Thank you so much. I appreciate your help. I'm sorry your kindness got you all dirty, though."

Aaron brushed at his pants and shrugged. "It'll wash. I'm glad I could help. Make sure you take her to the vet, though. Get her checked out."

"We will. She seems young enough, it'll be a couple of months before we'll need to get her spayed."

She helped Gideon get buckled into his booster seat and closed the door again. The kitten was content on his lap.

While she was turned away from him, Aaron spotted a leaf caught in her hair and some debris clinging to the back of her shoulder. Before he changed his mind, he took a step closer to her. "You have something in your hair. Here, let me get it for you."

She froze as he extracted the leaf, amazed that the silky strands were even softer than he'd imagined. He swept it to the side and lightly brushed off the debris.

The contact was brief, yet it felt as though it'd seared his skin. He cleared his throat and took a step back. "There you go."

"Thank you." She turned around slowly and clasped her hands tightly in front of her.

Aaron glanced at the sky, the storm front moving steadily closer. "You'd better get going or you'll get caught in the rain." They both needed an escape from the moment — from whatever it was that'd just happened. Was he the only one affected? The questioning look in her eyes said he wasn't, or maybe that was wishful thinking.

Either way, she broke eye contact. "Same with you. Thanks again for your help. With everything."

"You're welcome." He lifted a hand in farewell and watched as she climbed into her vehicle and disappeared across the parking lot.

The image of her shapely legs sticking out from underneath the car and the way her eyes had reflected the clouds in the sky didn't come close to disappearing from his mind.

~

Serenity and Gideon ducked into a pet store on the way home to get a few supplies. She bought a pan for a litterbox, a small thing of litter, and a little bag of cat food. Her limited funds didn't allow for anything else and she'd already determined to use dishes they owned to hold the food and water.

By the time they got home, the storm was upon them and rain came down in sheets. She rushed Gideon and the kitten in before going back to get everything else.

They changed into dry clothes and set up the litterbox, food, and water before the kitten got any ideas on somewhere else to do her business. The little thing appeared grateful and used her new facilities immediately.

At least she appeared clean, especially after getting wet in the rain. Serenity would have to see how she was going to squeeze a vet visit into their budget.

Gideon stretched out on the floor, rested his chin on an arm, and watched as the kitten started to eat. The smile on his face told her she'd done the right thing by bringing the little animal home.

Her mind flew to Aaron and the way he'd looked, holding the kitten in his large hands. A tickle on her shoulder blade made her shiver. Even though she was still cold from getting soaked in the rain, she could have sworn some residual warmth from his touch remained. She caught a hint of his aftershave — something woodsy and unforgettable.

She rotated her shoulders in an attempt to push the thoughts from her mind. The guy had an amazing singing voice, he was friendly, he taught music to special needs children, and he rescued kittens.

Serenity frowned. Seriously, there had to be a catch. There was always a catch.

Chapter Eight

D id you get the kitten settled in okay last night?" Aaron paused at the table where he and Serenity usually ate lunch. He didn't see her when he got to work and had been looking forward to the break all morning.

Serenity smiled up at him. "We did. I've only ever had dogs. Let me just say that a cat is a lot easier to litterbox train than a dog is to house train."

Her chuckle brought a smile to his face. There was something about her laugh that always made him want to join in. Her hair fell loose down her back. He remembered what it was like to touch it the day before and flexed his hand.

"I'm glad to hear it. And was Gideon as excited about the cat after you got her home?" He slid into the chair across from her, setting the bag of food down on the floor at his feet.

"Oh, yes. He didn't leave her side until I insisted it was time for bed. She slept with him last night."

Aaron thought about Gideon and somehow the

interaction didn't surprise him. He was still trying to get to know the boy, but had discovered several times that Gideon would become concerned if another child in his class got upset. He could see how caring for a kitten would be good for him. "Did you name her?"

"I went with Kia. It seemed fitting."

He laughed. "That's a perfect name." He took in the plain sandwich that was still wrapped in front of her and the little bag of chips. She'd eaten the same thing for lunch since the first time he sat down with her in the breakroom. She usually didn't seem to mind, but he'd caught a wishful look on her face a time or two when he brought leftovers.

When he had a few extra minutes, he decided to get takeout from one of the popular Mexican restaurants in town. He reached across the table and moved her food to the side, setting the bag down between them.

Her eyes widened as she took in the bag and then studied him. "What's this?"

"Lunch." He suppressed a grin at the confused expression on her face. He got a couple of paper plates out of a cabinet and handed her one.

"You bought me lunch?"

"You've got to have a break from sandwiches. Please tell me you eat something else at home."

Her cheeks grew pink. "We do. Funds are a bit limited right now. But we eat and that's more than good enough." She took in a deep breath and her stomach let out a long growl. Her face went from red to crimson.

Aaron laughed loudly. He pulled out a stack of tortillas and a container with grilled chicken and vegetables, refried beans, rice, and toppings. "This place makes some of the best chicken fajitas in town."

He pushed the tortillas towards her. "Dig in."

Her hesitation was momentary before she did just as he asked. When she'd rolled everything up in the tortilla and taken a bite, her eyes closed and she moaned. "You weren't kidding. These are amazing."

He took a big bite and nodded his satisfaction. This was a good call. After polishing his fajita off in a few bites, he rolled up another one. He was even happier to see that Serenity ate a second fajita as well.

When she leaned back in her chair and rested her hands on her stomach, her eyes twinkled. "Thank you. Now I don't have to eat for a week."

Aaron raised an eyebrow at her. "They're good, but not that good. And you're welcome." He made a third fajita. "Who knows, maybe I'll bring some again next week, Tuesday instead. Isn't Taco Tuesday a thing?" He winked. Serenity gave him a warning look but said nothing. He chose to take that as agreement. "What are your hobbies?"

She blinked at him as though he'd asked a question in another language. He hadn't expected her hesitation over what he thought was a simple inquiry.

Serenity tapped the cover of the book on the table near her. "I read. Does that count?"

"Absolutely."

"What about you?"

The words came quickly and he suspected she was trying to deflect the conversation from herself. He thought about asking her what types of books she liked to read, but decided to go with her distraction.

"Most of what I do is music-related. My job here plus playing at church. There's a group of guys there that I play basketball with occasionally. Not that I'm great, but it's fun. Do you play?"

"I don't. Or at least I haven't for a long time. It's funny because my brother and sister do. They're always trying to convince me to join them. Now that they're both married, they've got two on two. They don't need a fifth."

Serenity stopped talking suddenly and Aaron suspected she hadn't meant to give quite as many details. He had the feeling she didn't experience a lot of fun in her life.

The need to replace the frown on her face with a smile was so strong, he knew he ought to put some distance between them. Especially with Cynthia's blasted guidelines hanging over their heads. But there was something about Serenity and the way he was drawn to her that refused to let him do that.

"Well, maybe it's time you played again." He gave her a wink. "I'll let you know the next time we throw a game together."

~

It was Friday night and Serenity was lounging on her futon, a book discarded next to her. Gideon was in bed and Kia was curled up in a little black ball between her ankles. She let her cell phone rest against her ear. "Do you want to hear something funny?"

"What's that?" Lexi managed to get the words out before she started coughing.

"Are you sure you're okay?"

"You sound like Lance. I'm fine. It's a head cold."

Serenity knew that but worried anyway. It was hard not to, especially after witnessing all her sister went through last year. She mentally prayed and released her fears. Or at least the bulk of them. "I know. You'd better make sure you get some extra rest."

"Yes, Mom." The sound of Lexi blowing her nose came across the phone. "Sorry. What's funny?"

"I'm bored. I can't remember the last time I was bored." Serenity laughed, the sound disrupting Kia. The kitten yawned widely, stretched her paws out, and then curled up again.

"I'd say that's a good thing. You've been so busy working that you haven't really had a life."

"Gee, thanks for that." Serenity rolled her eyes and blew out a puff of air. "I've been reading a lot."

"And that's great. But you need a hobby."

Was it a bad sign that the second person in as many days was commenting on her pathetic existence? She wanted to get annoyed at Lexi, but it was hard to do when she wasn't wrong.

"What do you suggest?"

"Besides finding yourself a handsome man so you can start dating?"

The first thing that came to Serenity's mind was a certain Music Man with piercing blue eyes. She sat up quickly, the movement disturbing Kia. She stood lazily, shot Serenity a nasty glare, and jumped to the floor.

"Yes, besides that."

Lexi laughed, the sound flowing into a cough. When it had quieted, she said, "You used to crochet. Do you remember that? You could pick it up again. We can always use tiny hats for the preemies here at the hospital. Maybe you could start up an online store and make a little side money."

"Are you serious? I haven't crocheted since I was fifteen."

"I thought you were bored. YouTube has a wealth of tutorials." Lexi started coughing again.

Serenity had to admit the idea held some appeal. She could make gifts for her family for Christmas in a few months.

"Listen, Lexi. You need to go and get some rest. That cough sounds horrible. Are you sure you don't need to see a doctor?"

There was a pause and she could hear the exchange of voices before Lexi came back on the line. "I'm sure, but Lance is insisting. He has an appointment for me tomorrow afternoon."

Lance must have taken the phone from her because his voice reached Serenity's ear. "Tell her, if she doesn't go to the doctor willingly, I'll pick her up and carry her there myself."

Serenity chuckled. "I'll do it. You're a good guy, Lance."

"Make sure to pass that along, too."

She was still laughing when Lexi got her phone back. "Go to the doctor. It doesn't hurt. Get some meds and get to feeling better, huh?"

"I will. I'll talk to you soon."

"You bet. Love you."

"I love you, too."

Serenity slid her phone onto the coffee table. The moment she did, Kia jumped back up on her lap, purring as she rubbed her head against Serenity's arm.

"What do you think? Should I get some yarn and learn to crochet? I bet you'd like a ball of yarn, no matter what I do with it, wouldn't you?"

Kia continued to purr as she curled up on Serenity's stomach, apparently content right where she was.

Serenity's mind drifted to the other suggestion Lexi had made. She chuckled when she thought about what her sister would have said if she'd known about Aaron.

She would insist Serenity bring him to a family night dinner. While she'd have to endure Tuck and Lance questioning him, it would be Lexi dropping hints about a happily-ever-after. And that was the last thing she needed right now. It was definitely better that she kept Aaron to herself.

Chapter Nine

Ever since the air conditioner went out yesterday morning, their place had been uncomfortably hot. Tired of sweating, Serenity suggested they get out for a while and Gideon had responded by shoving his feet into his shoes and running to the door.

Serenity walked into the craft store and welcomed the air conditioning as the doors slid shut behind them. She couldn't remember the last time she'd been in a place like this. By the fascinated look on Gideon's face, she wasn't sure he ever had.

From the giant fall display in the middle of the entrance to the floor-to-ceiling shelves containing more pumpkins and scarecrows, it was the most she'd ever seen in one place. It would be easy to get lost browsing this Sunday afternoon. Especially when she wasn't in a hurry to get home.

Gideon climbed into the main part of a shopping basket and they headed towards the back of the store in search of yarn. It took ten minutes to locate it, but then she stood in awe at the three aisles of yarn in every weight and color.

Gideon reached for a skein of neon red. "Not that one, big guy." Under her guidance, they chose several colors together. A few crochet hooks and some tapestry needles later and she was more than ready to escape yarntopia.

Focusing closely on maneuvering the basket through the large displays of glass vases and objects, she hadn't expected Gideon to stand up quickly and start gesturing down an aisle.

"Sit down. You're going to make me crash the basket." Which, judging by the way the displays were set up, would have resulted in a domino effect. It might be cool to see, but really rough on the wallet.

She lifted him out of the basket and followed him over to a kit for a robotic train.

"I didn't expect to see the two of you here."

Serenity whipped around and ran right into Aaron's solid chest. The blue hand basket he'd been holding clattered to the floor at their feet. His arms came around her, keeping her steady, and she was close enough to feel the vibrations from his chuckle.

"You scared me!" Her voice sounded more like a squeak.

"Sorry." But he didn't seem all that apologetic. His blue eyes changed to a darker cobalt and humor gave them a twinkle. It was a combination that made it nearly impossible to move.

It took everything in her, but she managed a shaky breath and a step backwards, despite the fact that it was the last thing she wanted to do.

The smile he gave her caused her stomach to flip flop. She cleared her throat. "Do you browse hobby stores often?"

"I frequent the toy aisle here, anyway." He winked. "Seriously, though, I find some great music-related toys here for my classroom." Aaron pointed to the display near Gideon. There were kazoos, harmonicas, finger cymbals, and a variety of other small instruments. "When someone has a birthday, I like to give them a kazoo or something like that. I realized today how low my stockpile was getting." He placed a handful of them and several other items into the basket and picked it up again. "What about you?"

Serenity tipped her head towards her shopping cart. "I used to crochet when I was a teenager. I thought I might try to expand my meager list of hobbies."

"Impressive."

She lifted her shoulders and let them fall again. "My sister volunteers at the Kitner hospital working with premature babies. She said they could use little hats for them. I thought it would be a good thing to start off with. Assuming I can pick it up again."

"I'm sure it'll be second nature in no time. And I would agree about it being a great use of your skills." There was that smile again, the one that took her heart rate and kicked it up a notch. Or two or three.

"Mostly we're trying to find places to go today where it's cool. Our air conditioner is out."

Aaron's brow wrinkled. "You're renting, right? Did you call the landlord?"

Serenity sighed. "Yep. But since it's the weekend, he said the earliest he can have someone come and fix it is Tuesday afternoon." She pressed her lips together. "It's going to be a long couple of days. We're taking our time here, may try to get a bite to eat somewhere, and then head to the store. At least we'll get our exercise." She wasn't overly excited about staying out all day. But it was a whole lot better than sweating it out for hours at home. Besides, after trying to get through yesterday, she planned to pick up a fan before heading home again.

~

Aaron couldn't believe the landlord wasn't going to do something about the air conditioning. "Tuesday? That's not good. It's ninety-eight degrees out there." If it were him, he'd make sure someone was there to fix it first thing Monday morning. Especially with a kid in the house. "You ought to call him again tomorrow and remind him. Or at least get an update."

She shuffled her feet. "I might. I don't want to be one of those needy renters, you know?"

"Calling to have trim nailed down might be needy. This is a different thing entirely." She said nothing and he suspected she was going to wait on the landlord's timeframe regardless of what he said.

Gideon tugged on Serenity's hand and signed that he was hungry. She smiled at him. "It is about time for lunch, isn't it? What do you say to burgers and fries?" The boy grinned. Serenity turned to Aaron. "Have you tried that burger place across the parking lot? Do they have French fries?"

"It's quite good and yes, they have fries. Three kinds, actually."

"Okay, good. There's a place in Kitner that only offers chips with their burgers." She jabbed a thumb in her son's direction. "That doesn't work so well for us."

Gideon knocked a box off the shelf and Serenity moved to help him. Aaron quickly centered his thoughts. Running into the pair of them was the last thing he'd expected when he'd turned down the aisle. Now they were all he could think about.

He pictured them baking in their house and it kept getting to him. They needed someone to fix their air conditioning as soon as possible. If he knew who her landlord was, he'd be tempted to call himself. He shoved the idea from his mind. The last thing he needed was to get personally involved in Serenity's life. The less he knew about her, the easier it'd be to keep his distance. He needed that line to stay firmly drawn in the sand. Besides, she'd made it clear she was fine waiting until Tuesday. He was better off leaving well enough alone.

Serenity reached down and straightened one of Gideon's sleeves, unrolling it so that it matched the other. Then she used her fingers to tickle him briefly, eliciting giggles from the boy.

A whisper of a wish passed through him. How was he supposed to keep his distance when he felt his entire being pulled towards her? He needed to leave now, before his heart stomped his logic into the ground. "I should probably ..."

Her lashes lifted as she straightened, a smile on her face.

His mouth went dry.

"Probably what?"

Pull her into his arms? Bury his face in her lilac-scented hair? He wiped his sweaty palms on his jeans. Clearly, he should have gotten off this highway some time ago — preferably taking the same exit his sanity had chosen. What was his deal? "Oh... to get something to eat."

Serenity pushed some hair away from her face with long, graceful fingers. "I hear you. We're starving. I think we're going to head out of here." She stopped, slipping her hands into her back pockets. "You're welcome to join us if you'd like."

She wanted him to go with them? Standing next to her in the middle of a hobby store was hard enough. If she continued to peek at him from beneath those long eyelashes…Did she have any idea how cute she was right now? He forced his gaze to take in the content of his basket. "You guys are having fun. I don't want to…"

Gideon grabbed his hand and tried to pull him towards the exit, a grin lighting up his face.

Now how was he supposed to say no to that? Aaron took a quick step to keep his balance. "Whoa, kiddo." Letting out a breath, he met her eyes and smiled. It was just lunch, right? They'd pay for their own meals and it wouldn't be that much different than if they'd run into each other there instead of the craft store.

Serenity waited for his reply, her face a jumble of emotions. Was she hoping he'd say yes or decline the invitation? He finally acquiesced with a quick dip of his chin. "It is one of the best burger places in town."

She led the way to the front of the store, Gideon standing on the back of the basket, his smaller hands grasping the handle between hers. If the two of them pulled on his heartstrings any more, he'd be lucky to survive the meal without doing something he'd beat himself up over later. He dug his wallet out of his back pocket and sighed. This would've been much simpler if he'd come by the craft store Friday after work like he'd originally planned.

But even as the thought took form, it dissipated like smoke when the sound of Serenity and Gideon laughing floated back to him. His heart swelled.

They paid for their items before driving to the burger joint and parking their cars in adjacent spots. Gideon held onto his mom's hand and, to Aaron's surprise, he reached out and took one of his as well.

Seeing the smile on Gideon's face reminded him so much of Kenneth, he could almost hear his little brother's voice. Memories Aaron had kept buried for years rushed to the surface. Holding one of his mother's hands while Kenneth held the other. The happiness on her face as she swung their arms back and forth. The sounds of both of them laughing as she tickled their bellies.

When he saw his mother now, it was difficult to imagine she was the same woman. He shook himself free of the thoughts, hating the swirl of emotion they always dredged up.

Serenity glanced over the menu that hung on the wall above the cash registers. Her brow wrinkled and she clasped her hands tightly together. When she stepped forward to place her order, she chose two of the most inexpensive meals on the menu. Aaron followed, ordering a double cheeseburger meal.

After they paid for their lunches, they claimed a table next to three arcade games. Gideon excitedly slid into one of the seats and grasped the steering wheel.

Serenity smiled at her son. "He loves these things and doesn't care a bit that I've never put money into one."

Aaron laughed. "I remember doing the same as a boy." He had a question that'd been plaguing him for a while. The words spilled out of his mouth before he could stop them. "Is Gideon's dad in the picture?" Yeah, that was smooth. But he'd gone over the question in his head a million times and couldn't think of a better way to ask. Blunt it was. He said a silent prayer that he hadn't offended her.

She took a long drink of her soda. He wasn't sure she was going to answer his question when she drew a deep breath and pinned him with her gaze.

"Jay never met Gideon. Getting pregnant during our senior year of high school wasn't part of the plan. He left before Gideon was born and relinquished all rights the following month."

The way she worked her jaw told Aaron she still resented Jay — maybe even hated him. He realized his fists were clenched and consciously made an effort to relax them.

She was silent a moment before continuing. "I was only eighteen. I suppose the stress of a pregnant girlfriend was more than he cared to deal with." She shrugged, as though it hadn't bothered her.

Aaron knew better. "What he did wasn't okay. I can't imagine walking away from my child like that."

She kept her gaze straight ahead but there was no missing the moisture that had gathered in her eyes. "Thank you." She swallowed hard. "I'm blessed to have a supportive family and an older brother who's great with Gideon. It's not the same as having a father, but a whole lot better than anything Jay might have attempted to do." She paused. "I'm sorry. When you asked, I imagine this was way more information than you were expecting."

She paid an unusual amount of attention to the straw paper she held in her hand. If she didn't normally tell people about Jay, he wondered if this meant she trusted him, even if just a little. She had to trust someone. "It sounds like you have a lot of family. Who's your best friend?" He watched the range of emotions on her face.

"Probably my siblings, Tuck and Lexi. I don't have any friends left from school. Having a baby as a senior will do that for you." She laughed, but there was no humor in the sound.

His chest tightened as sadness shadowed her face. When Jay walked away, he must've stepped all over Serenity in the process. At twenty-three or twenty-four, she was way too young to be this sad and jaded. Not only was she raising a son on her own, but she'd given up her family's support system in order to provide him with a better education and therapy opportunities. Didn't Serenity realize how strong she truly was? Not everyone in her position would have been as brave. As far as he was concerned, she deserved the title of Super Woman.

Aaron released his drink, his hands damp from the condensation, and dried them off on a napkin. He'd kept his distance from women for a reason. After Kenneth died, he had to watch his parents' relationship fall apart. The fights that eventually ended in divorce were more than enough motivation for him to steer clear of relationships. His life — his job and the kids he worked with — they'd been sufficient.

Until now. Meeting Serenity made him wonder if things could be different. Better.

A reminder of Cynthia's stupid memo punched a hole in his thoughts. He exhaled, his breath moving the napkin on the table. The professional boundaries were probably a good thing. It'd keep them both from getting hurt. Serenity needed a friend here, not more heartache to add to what she'd already endured.

He glanced up at her. Her eyes were a window to the sadness that remained inside her. If he could make things better for her, he would. "I'm sorry Jay hurt you. He walked away from a good thing."

She nodded slowly. "Gideon's a great kid. I doubt Jay will ever realize how much he's missing out on."

"Agreed. Though I wasn't just talking about Gideon."

Aaron focused his attention on the food arriving at their table, but he could see Serenity's head turn in his direction. There was no missing the flush of color that crept into her face while his own pulse was pounding in his ears. He'd meant to comfort her, and instead he'd made things worse. This was exactly why he needed to keep his distance.

Thankful for the distraction that distributing the food allowed, Aaron slid a basket of fries and a burger in front of each of them. Serenity called Gideon over and he happily climbed into his seat. He promptly opened his burger, handed the meat to his mom, and proceeded to pile French fries in its place. Aaron chuckled when Gideon put the top bun on and took a large bite of his new sandwich.

Serenity rubbed her son's hair affectionately. "He's done that for a couple of years now. I can't get him to eat hamburger for anything. I, on the other hand, have no problem with it." She took an exaggerated bite of her own burger.

Aaron laughed loudly then. "A healthy appetite — there's nothing wrong with that." She licked a bit of ketchup off her lip, completely distracting him from his own meal. He had to bring his train of thought and the conversation to a much safer topic.

"Your brother's older than you? Is he married?"

"Yes, he's five years older than I am. He and Laurie have been married a year. He's a police officer with the force in Kitner. Tuck's ex-partner, Lance, married my sister, Lexi, this March. Lance runs his dad's carpentry business now."

He'd have to remember to never make her family mad. Aaron tried to imagine what his relationship with his brother might be like now if they'd been given the chance. It was nearly impossible to do. He envied Serenity her siblings.

"What about you?" Serenity asked. Some melted cheese stuck to a finger and she wiped it off on a napkin. "Do you have family nearby?"

He always dreaded that question. How did one explain that, no matter how close he was in proximity to his family, they were always worlds apart?

Chapter Ten

S erenity saw Aaron's hesitation about his family. It'd seemed like a natural thing to ask when they'd been talking about her own. She watched as Aaron finished his burger and worked to polish off the last of his fries. He was dipping them, two at a time, into ketchup. She hid a grin when she realized Gideon ate his own fries in the exact same way. She suppressed the urge to pull her cell phone out and snap a picture.

Aaron brushed the salt off his hands and cleared his throat. "No, I don't have family around here. My parents divorced when I was twelve. Now my mom lives in New York and my dad in California. I see each of them maybe once a year, and never together."

The words were said matter-of-factly with little emotion. Her surprise must have shone on her face because he held up a hand as though it would halt her train of thought.

"Trust me, it's better that way. I had a younger brother who passed away and neither of them were able to move past it. Things were rough until they split and they're still volatile when we all get together, even now. It's not worth it."

Serenity hadn't expected that and worked to digest his words. Should she ask him about his brother? Avoid the subject completely? The strangely emotion-free expression on his face wasn't giving her much of a clue.

Gideon motioned to the arcade, interrupting the awkward haze that had descended over the table. Serenity nodded. "If you're done, you can go play. Let's wipe the grease off your hands first." She did that and smiled as he ran back to the car game. The insistent beeping from a fryer in the back of the restaurant joined the sound of the bell as the front door swung open. "I'm sorry it's like that with your parents. And I'm really sorry about your brother. I can't even imagine." She didn't know what else to say.

He must have taken pity on her — or maybe he took advantage of the moment to change topics — and turned the conversation back to her. "What about your parents? Do they get along?"

"Yes, they were best friends. My parents always got along great and when my dad died a few years ago, it was devastating for Mom."

"I'm sorry." A flash of pain appeared in his blue eyes, gone a mere moment later. It was replaced with the kind of understanding only someone else who'd lost a close loved one could express. "What happened?"

"He passed after a long battle with pancreatic cancer." Even years later, thinking about Dad made her heart hurt. When Lexi was diagnosed with ovarian cancer, it was like reliving those moments. Praise God He was able to use surgery, chemotherapy, and some natural remedies to help her beat it. The image of Aaron wavered and morphed as tears filled her eyes.

"That had to be rough. I'm sorry your family had to go through it." When he cupped his hand over hers, they both froze in place.

A surge of adrenaline began where he touched her and flowed through her body, leaving her head buzzing from the jolt. They stared at their joined hands for several breaths before Aaron pulled his back.

She shifted in her chair. "I appreciate it. We were all able to be with him at the end and I'm thankful for that." Somehow, she'd managed to keep her voice from shaking.

"I'm glad." He reached for his drink but stalled, moving to crumple his napkin into a tiny ball and dropping it into the basket the food had come in. "Saying goodbye is never easy."

The air felt heavy as crackles of awkwardness and uncertainty arched between them. Serenity could still feel Aaron's hand on hers as though the contact had seared her skin. She rubbed her palms together several times and leaned in her chair towards Gideon.

"Hey, big guy. Five more minutes and then it's time to go." He shook his head, never taking his attention off the game he was watching. "Yes, five minutes. We need to go get a fan. We're going to set it up in your room and Mommy's going to camp out there tonight. Remember?" She made a note of the time on her watch.

Ugh, she wasn't looking forward to getting back to their house and the sweltering heat she knew was waiting for them. It'd be worth going into work tomorrow for the air conditioning alone.

Aaron asked if she'd like a refill of her drink. She

told him she would. He gathered the trash and disposed of it before taking her cup to the dispenser. Serenity watched as he chose the cola and realized she'd never told him what she'd been drinking. It was such a small thing and yet Serenity found his attention to detail nestled itself in her heart. She took the cup from him, their fingers touching momentarily.

She fought to keep from reacting to the connection, moving quickly to tell Gideon it was time to go. She took her son by the hand and led the way back out to the parking lot, Aaron close behind them.

Serenity turned the car and air conditioner on, got Gideon buckled in, and faced Aaron. "I'm glad you could join us. Don't tell Letty, but I think you're Gideon's favorite teacher. You made his day." And hers, too, but she wasn't about to tell him that. Especially when simply thinking it made her face warm.

Aaron grinned at Gideon and gave him a wave. "He's a great kid. I'm glad he's in my class, he's a lot of fun to teach." His eyes moved from the window to her face, concern flashing across his features. He pinched the skin above his Adam's apple. "I hate the idea of you guys going back to your house without the A/C. I can come and check it if you want. I'm no mechanic, but if it's something simple, maybe I can help."

He was offering to come to her house and attempt to fix her air conditioner? If there was even a possibility he would be successful, she wanted to jump at the opportunity. But with his hands now buried deep in his pockets and the way he kept looking at everything but her, he acted like he was waiting to be sent behind enemy lines. She didn't need his help if he had some misguided sense of responsibility.

"I appreciate the offer. But I'm sure you have other things to do on a Sunday afternoon." His presence alone was making her jittery. She prayed he couldn't tell. "We should let you get back to your plans."

Aaron adopted a wide stance and met her gaze head-on. "It'll only take a moment. If it's something easy to fix, you won't have to deal with the heat for the next forty-eight hours or more." His jaw clenched, the muscles flexing.

His eyes held hers until she finally nodded her agreement. "Do you want to follow us over there?"

"Sure. Lead the way."

Serenity whirled and pulled the car door open and got inside. Once she was safe within the confines of her vehicle, she released a shaky breath and rolled her eyes. How did one handsome man manage to throw her entire world off kilter with a single look? She adjusted the nearest vent so the cold air blew directly onto her face before putting the car in drive.

~

Aaron kept Serenity's Kia in sight as they followed traffic several streets over and into a neighborhood consisting mostly of apartment buildings. He parked behind her and got out, taking in details of the duplex. It wasn't bad, but it could use a new coat of paint in the near future. What little grass there was in the front was going to need to be mowed soon. Since it was only Serenity and Gideon living there, he assumed she must go out and do that herself. While he had no doubt she was more than capable, he hated the idea of her pushing the mower in the summer sun.

Serenity turned the key in the lock. "Watch out for

Kia. She likes to try and dart out if we're not careful." She pushed the door open, moving a leg to block the narrow gap. As if on cue, Kia stumbled against it. Serenity scooped the kitten up in one arm. "Where do you think you're going? No, Ma'am."

Aaron stepped over the threshold and shut the door behind him. The stuffy heat of the house closed in. He had no doubt that he'd made the right decision offering to try and fix the air conditioning unit. He wouldn't have been able to knowingly leave anyone like this without trying to help first.

Gideon kicked his shoes off and ran into another room. Serenity led Aaron to a door in the hallway. "Here's the A/C and the thermostat is on the wall over there. I'll be right back. I'm going to make sure Kia still has enough water after being stuck in here like this."

He observed her as she buried her face in the kitten's fur before walking towards the kitchen. Unable to take his eyes off her retreating form until she disappeared, he took a deep breath and focused on the problem he might actually have a shot at fixing.

There were no obvious issues that he could detect. When Serenity returned, she stood against a wall and observed, her arms crossed in front of her.

Aaron messed with the thermostat and finally decided to check on the condenser outside. She showed him to the back door. When he approached the unit, he had a good idea what the problem was. He headed back inside ten minutes later.

Serenity met him in the hallway. "Did you find anything?" She bit her lip as hope shined in her eyes.

"I might have. Let me test something real quick." He strode to the thermostat, turned it back on, and grinned with satisfaction when cool air flowed from the vents.

"You actually fixed it!"

Aaron's heart stuttered as she flashed him a smile bright enough to rival the sun. Heat that had nothing to do with the temperature of the room climbed the back of his neck. He laughed nervously. "You don't have to sound so surprised."

She considered him for a moment. He sensed she wanted to say something. She'd moved to stand under one of the A/C vents and the current of air blew stray strands of hair around her face. Several caught on her cheek and he resisted the urge to sweep them away. Maybe even let his hand linger on her face to see if the skin there was as soft as it appeared…

Aaron forced his gaze away from her and focus on the number of pictures that hung on the wall. His eyes were drawn to one photo in particular. Serenity was sitting in a rocking chair with Gideon curled up on her lap. She was reading to him and both seemed content — as if there were nowhere else in the world either of them would rather be. "This is a sweet image."

Serenity grinned. "Thank you. My sister-in-law, Laurie, took it. It's my favorite picture of us." Gideon ran into the room, all smiles, and pointed to the vent. Serenity picked him up. "Isn't it great? The Music Man fixed it for us. I'm starting to wonder if there's anything he can't do."

Her words lodged themselves in his heart. As mother and son danced in the cool air, the boy's laughter filled the room. Aaron's chest grew tight. The need to be a part of this scene as more than a bystander was beyond what he could take. He had to get out of there.

"It really was nothing. There's a small leak in the

hose leading to the condenser. The grass was growing a lot faster in that area thanks to the extra moisture and it was blocking the air intake. When your landlord does send someone on Tuesday, mention that hole. I cleared away the grass for you, so you should be good to go after that." He took several steps towards the front door and his escape.

Serenity slid Gideon to the floor again and put her hands on her son's shoulders. "What you did wasn't nothing, Aaron. Thank you for being our hero today."

He swallowed hard, nodded in what he hoped was an acceptable response, and reached for the doorknob. "With any luck, the house will cool down quickly. I'd better get going. See you guys tomorrow."

He gave them a quick wave and darted outside. He got settled in his car and groaned. There were no regrets about coming and fixing her A/C. But he was going to have to be real careful about how much time he spent around Serenity and her son.

The sound of her sweet voice calling him a hero kept replaying in his head and every time, his chest constricted in response.

Right now, he'd do almost anything to be the kind of man she needed. The realization hit him like a punch to the gut. He pulled away from their house, knowing it was a risk he shouldn't take. For their sakes as much as his own.

Chapter Eleven

onday morning, Serenity got Gideon settled in his classroom and then made her way to the front office. The moment she stepped foot in the room, the sight of Maggie was as effective as lead weights in her shoes might have been. She stopped, her jaw dropping.

Maggie noticed her and stood. She turned slowly with her arms out to the sides. "What do you think? I thought I'd try something new. Yay or nay?"

Serenity took in the dress that was the same yellow as the neon sign for the diner down the street. The combination of it plus the numerous matching streaks in Maggie's hair was enough to make her wish she'd brought sunglasses. What did she think? Colorful. Headache-inducing. "It's cheerful." That sounded a little better, right? "What inspired it?"

"I saw a patch of sunflowers. They always make me smile and I thought to myself, 'Why not bring that happiness to work with me?' And here I am."

And how was she supposed to argue with that? She

couldn't, so she took her seat and leafed through papers from the metal rack. Tammy had started placing them there as a to-do list of sorts. Serenity didn't mind.

Parents brought their children in to start the school day and Serenity often had to fight back the grin that threatened to break free when several of the parents gawked at Maggie.

She wasn't sure if Maggie didn't notice, or if she assumed they were soaking in the happy flower vibe.

Once the morning rush cleared out, the rest of the time dragged. Serenity had thought of little else besides Aaron and how he'd taken the time to come fix her A/C the day before. Couple that with the way he'd touched her hand and yeah, it was more than a little distracting.

She'd spent most of yesterday evening trying to figure out what she could do to thank him for his kindness. After agonizing over it for way longer than she should have, she decided to bake a batch of cookies. Hopefully Aaron liked chocolate chip as much as Tuck did. The toe of her shoe touched the plastic container filled with them that she'd stashed under the desk.

She'd hoped to catch a glimpse of him that morning and finally resigned herself to wait until lunch at one. Simply thinking about it resulted in a fluttering in her stomach. Was Aaron looking forward to it like she was?

Maggie's voice broke through her thoughts. "Did you see Crazy Day on the calendar for tomorrow?"

"Oh! Thanks for reminding me. I was going to ask about that. Do I dress Gideon in something silly?"

"Most of the kids come in with mismatched clothes and something funny done to their hair." A mischievous glint appeared in Maggie's eyes. She glanced around to make sure no one would overhear their conversation. "I usually do something fun for that day, too. But I had an idea this morning for something we could both do. It'd be good for some laughs."

Serenity took in the other woman's appearance, wondering how much crazier she could look. But as Maggie described her idea, Serenity had to admit it was a good one. When she agreed, Maggie clasped her hands together. They spent the next thirty minutes going over the details.

Several hours later, when it was finally time for lunch, Serenity arranged her food on a paper towel at her usual table. She'd been anxious to see Aaron and give him the cookies all morning. When he never showed up, her disappointment was like a sharp knife that sliced through her appetite and left her spending most of her break glancing at the door.

It wasn't like this was the first lunch they'd eaten apart. She knew things came up. Even she had to take a lunch last week for a dental appointment. Regardless of what her common sense told her, she found herself running through everything that happened the day before. She'd truly enjoyed their time together and she was pretty sure Aaron felt the same spark of attraction she had.

Maybe she'd misinterpreted his actions? What if yesterday had left him so uncomfortable, he was avoiding her today? The thought brought together a tangle of nerves in her stomach.

Serenity did her best to finish her lunch and went back to work. By the end of the day, she was more than ready to escape and get home. She was holding Gideon's hand and walking across the parking lot when she spotted Aaron just ahead. Should she say hello or keep going? The question left her glued in place when he turned and spotted them.

A hand raised in greeting, he approached them. "Hey, you two. Heading home?"

Serenity forced a friendly smile. "We are. It's been a true Monday. I hope your day went smoothly."

Aaron gave a half shrug. "I had an appointment this morning that got pushed back to one." His gaze locked with hers. "I missed seeing you at lunch."

"You did?" Serenity kicked herself for sounding pathetic. "I'm sorry about the meeting. That's never fun. I missed seeing you at lunch, too." She pulled the container of cookies out of her bag. "I brought these for you."

"What's this for?" He tapped the top of the container as he took it from her.

"It's a thank you for going out of your way to fix our A/C. I can't express how glad I am — and Gideon, too."

She watched nervously as he opened it. He pulled a cookie out and popped it into his mouth. "Mmmmm…" He finished it and smiled at her. "Now that's one of the best chocolate chip cookies I've ever had. Did you make them yourself?"

"I did." Serenity's face heated up and she leaned down to remove an imaginary speck of dirt from Gideon's shirt.

"These are completely unnecessary, but thank you."

A chuckle escaped her throat and she shook her head. "You know, I put on a brave front yesterday. But I wasn't looking forward to spending much time in that house without a working A/C. You were a huge blessing to us." Her eyes went to a lock of hair above one of his ears that had gotten mussed and was sticking out a little. Serenity was torn between thinking it was cute and wanting to reach across and fix it for him just so she could touch the subtle curl.

Aaron replaced the lid. "I'm glad I could help." He tipped his head towards the container. "If you ever need assistance in the future, all you have to do is holler. Especially if you pay in cookies." He looked like he wanted to say something else. Instead, he motioned in the direction of their car. "See you tomorrow?"

Serenity nodded. "Tomorrow." She took Gideon's hand again and continued their walk across the parking lot. She felt his blue eyes on her but refused to turn around and see if she was right.

He'd had a meeting today. That's why he hadn't been at lunch. It wasn't because he regretted spending the afternoon with them.

Relief flooded her system, quickly followed by annoyance. Since when did her entire day center on whether or not a guy wanted to eat lunch with her? How pathetic was she? She'd managed to eat hundreds of meals all on her own until now. If she continued to do so or not shouldn't make a difference.

Except that it did.

Serenity opened the car door and sank into the seat. As she watched Aaron's car weave its way through the parking lot and disappear, the truth wedged itself into her chest. Whether or not she wanted to admit it, spending time with him had become the highlight of her day.

~

Aaron passed through the front office Tuesday

morning, completely unaware of what was waiting for him. His feet stopped in their tracks and he took in the duo sitting behind the desk.

Maggie was dressed in a pair of jeans, a normal blouse, and her hair was brown. Just brown, with no streaks of color. He doubted it was her natural hair color.

Now Serenity, on the other hand, was wearing a bright floral skirt with a pink shirt that matched the blooms, and she had rainbow streaks in her hair.

The two women were watching him, matching amusement in their eyes.

Serenity's lips twitched. "It's Crazy Day. Didn't you hear?"

Aaron chuckled and shook his head at them. "I did. But for me, crazy is a pair of mismatched socks and shoes." He pulled the legs of his pants up to show off his clashing footwear. "I have to hand it to you two. If this were a contest, you'd be a shoe in for first prize."

The ladies laughed and he bid them goodbye, catching a last quick peek at Serenity before she disappeared from sight.

The carefree smile on her face stuck with him through the morning.

At lunch, he got Mexican food again and carried it into the breakroom. Serenity already had her sandwich out. "Didn't I tell you this was going to be Taco Tuesday from now on? Or some kind of Mexican food Tuesday, anyway." He took in her bright attire and grinned. "Or did you switch personalities with Maggie? Do you not like Mexican food now?"

"Maggie doesn't like tacos?"

He laughed. "I have no idea what Maggie does and doesn't like." He'd spent most of his time at the

Academy avoiding the woman and her flirting. Though, come to think of it, she'd done very little of it since Serenity had started working there.

Serenity quickly packaged up her lunch and made room for the taco combination plate he placed in front of her. "This smells amazing. Thank you."

"You're welcome." Aaron nodded at her hair. "Was this Maggie's idea, or yours?"

"It was hers, but I have to admit it's a good one. She came over to the house last night and brought the clothes and hair extensions. I loaned her one of my shirts." She tossed him a knowing look. "She's not as bad as you think she is. It's all exterior stuff. Inside, she's smart and funny." She chuckled, apparently remembering a previous conversation. "It's been a while since I've had this much fun. My sister says I'm too serious. That I don't relax and laugh enough. I've been thinking she's probably right."

"I'm glad — carefree looks good on you." He admired the long lashes that fell, blocking his view of her eyes. "What brought about this change?"

She peeked at him from beneath her eyelashes. "I think a lot of it has to do with the friends I'm around every day."

Aaron's heart stuttered and he suddenly wondered what Serenity truly considered him. Right then, he wished he could read her thoughts. He cleared his throat. "So those are hair extensions? I wasn't sure if it was that, or if you'd dyed your hair."

"Goodness, no. Though I'm thinking about getting it cut. I've had my hair long like this since before Gideon was born." She curled some of the hair around her finger. "Maybe it's about time I did something different."

Was she waiting for his opinion? He thought her hair was gorgeous. But if it were shorter, it would flow around her shoulders more and he liked that visual. He gave a brief nod. "I have no doubt your hair is beautiful no matter what you do with it — and that includes adding rainbow streaks." He gave her a wink. "But I think cutting it short would suit you well."

Her cheeks slowly shifted color until they matched her shirt. Aaron did his best to hide his grin as he dug into his lunch. Spending this hour with Serenity was the best part of his day.

Chapter Twelve

For Serenity, Fridays at Hope were usually busy — but in a good way. Everyone tended to be in a happy mood with the weekend on the horizon. But this particular Friday had started off poorly the moment she walked in the door.

The large printer quit working. She and Maggie spent the better part of an hour monkeying with it before admitting defeat and calling the company to come fix it. Cynthia wasn't happy about that at all, claiming she had a large project that needed to be printed right away. As if there was a thing Serenity could do about it.

Not long later, a parent yelled at Serenity for being unable to locate a permission slip. She tried not to take it personally because the mother was clearly having a bad day. It was a shame she felt she had to share.

Serenity sank into her chair at the same time that the front office door swung open. Letty led the way and held the door for Aaron who came through with Gideon in his arms.

Serenity jumped to her feet. The moment she saw the blood on his face, her stomach fell to the floor.

Nurse Candace ushered them into her room. "What happened?"

Gideon reached for Serenity and she eagerly took him into her arms. Letty kept a hand over the cloth on his forehead.

Letty's face was pale and her eyes wide. "He was playing out on the playground and jumped from the top of one of the ladders. He hit his head on one of the other pieces of equipment." Her free hand was shaking. "Aaron saw me in the hall and carried him the rest of the way."

Serenity had seen Gideon do that very thing many times before and had always told him he was going to wind up hurting himself.

Gideon was wailing, large tears escaping the corners of his eyes. Serenity brushed some hair away from the cloth and kissed his cheek. "Shhhh. Let's let Nurse Candace see you. Everything's going to be okay."

Without waiting for permission, Candace donned some gloves and took over. She pulled the cloth away from the wound. A lot of blood was on the fabric, but only a tiny amount continued to ooze.

Serenity fought not to react to the gash. The last thing she wanted was for Gideon to see her worry. His eyes stayed on her face and she smiled.

Aaron patted Gideon's knee. "You sure are a brave boy, Gideon."

Candace rubbed a thumb on his head. "It's true. You're one of the bravest kids I've had come in here, did you know that?"

He'd stopped crying and sniffed loudly.

Letty shivered. "I'm sorry this happened."

Serenity put a hand on her shoulder. "Are you kidding? I've watched him do the same thing. He's fearless. This isn't your fault."

Letty seemed relieved to know that Serenity wasn't going to blame her. But she continued to watch Gideon nervously. Aaron caught Serenity's eyes and gave her a reassuring smile.

Candace took some fresh gauze out of a pouch, put some antibiotic cream on it, and placed it back over the cut. She then used some white tape to keep it in place. "He's going to be fine, but that cut's big enough, I think you should take him in for stitches. Especially with it being right there on his forehead. He'll have a scar, but they'll keep it from being a huge one."

Serenity was nodding, but her hands felt numb. She'd never had to take Gideon to the hospital for any reason before. The first thing she wanted to do was call Lexi and ask her to stitch Gideon up. Or call Tuck and get him to go with them in case Gideon put up a fight. If he did that, how was she going to hold him still?

Tears built up in her eyes and she blinked them away. She would not let her little boy see her cry. Not when he needed her to be strong. She nodded firmly.

"Okay." She turned to retrieve her bag but Maggie was already there, holding it out to her. "Thank you." She slung it over her shoulder, and reached for Gideon. He wrapped his little arms around her neck as she lifted him off the table.

"You're welcome." Maggie rubbed the boy's back. "I'm sorry about your head. You get to feeling better, okay?"

Letty put a hand on Serenity's arm. "If you need anything at all, you'd better call me."

"I will, Letty. Thank you." Serenity's head lifted

when Aaron stopped in front of her.

"Do you want me to carry him out for you?"

"I've got him. We'll be fine." Her voice sounded wooden, even to her own ears.

"Then I'll walk out and help you get into the car. Here, hand me your keys."

Serenity obeyed. She thanked Candace and then walked quickly to the parking lot. On the way to her vehicle, Aaron told her the quickest way to the nearest hospital.

Serenity got Gideon settled and slid in behind the steering wheel. Thankfully, he'd stopped crying. She forced herself to focus on the road and finding the hospital.

Father God, please make this as easy as possible on him. I hate seeing my baby hurt.

~

Aaron got into his own vehicle and followed Serenity out of the parking lot. She'd made it pretty clear she intended to take Gideon to the ER herself. But he didn't buy it. Not after seeing the fear that worked its way into her eyes. She never had to go through things alone back home and he wasn't about to let her do it here, either.

He spoke with Maggie on the phone, letting her know his next class wasn't until three and he'd be back by then in case anyone was looking for him.

After Serenity parked her vehicle, he chose a nearby spot and went to see if he could help. She shot him a wary glare the moment she spotted him. He was prepared and ignored it completely.

Serenity eased Gideon out of the car and into her

arms. Aaron moved to shut the door behind them and followed them towards the ER entrance.

She peeked at him over the top of Gideon's head. "You didn't have to come. He's my son — I've got him."

He met her gaze without blinking. "I realize that. You have everything under control and Gideon's one lucky little boy to have a mom he can rely on to take care of him. I'm here for you, Serenity. I've got your back if you need anything."

Aaron could've sworn her eyes misted then, but she turned her attention to the sliding doors before he could be certain. Was she glad he didn't leave? Or was she upset with him? Right now, it didn't matter. He was confident she needed him, whether she realized it or not.

By some miracle, they only waited twenty minutes in the waiting area before being called back. Serenity didn't tell him otherwise so he joined them.

The nurse helped get Gideon set up on a bed with hanging curtains providing a degree of privacy. His body appeared tiny compared to the white sheets around him. His eyes were red-rimmed and dried blood all over his shirt bore evidence of his accident.

Serenity took a spot next to him, smoothing back his hair with one hand. "I hope they get him stitched up soon."

There was no mistaking the way her voice shook, or the way she kept her gaze on her son's face.

Gideon rested on the gurney, his eyes looked tired and he didn't move a lot. Aaron put a hand on his shoulder. "You're a brave kid. I'm proud of you." The boy lightly touched the gauze on his head. "I see that. I'll bet it hurt a bunch." The pout in response made

Aaron's heart ache. He left a hand there and reached over to cover one of Serenity's. "Everything's going to be fine."

She nodded. When she didn't look up, he gave her hand a squeeze until she lifted her gaze to his. "I'm okay. Just worried. I don't know how he's going to react to this. Normally my brother would be here to help if he fights the nurse. Or my sister would do the stitching herself." Tears glistened in her eyes. "I probably should have stayed in Kitner. Maybe leaving was a mistake."

Aaron knew that she was close to her family, but only now did he realize how much support she must have gotten for Gideon. To have people who had her back like that was hard to come by and it must have been difficult for her to walk away from it. He rubbed the top of her hand with his thumb before letting go. "I'm here and I'll help in any way I can."

Those brown eyes spoke her thanks even if she didn't utter a word.

A nurse came in with a set of scrubs that resembled a summer sky and wore a smile just as bright. "I'm here to patch this handsome little guy up."

The nurse explained everything as she went, showed the instruments to Gideon, and then gave a nod to Serenity when she was ready.

Aaron reached over to hold one of Gideon's hands while Serenity leaned down until her head was at his level. When the first shot went into the skin to help deaden the area for stitches, the poor little boy cringed and cried out as his body tensed.

"Baby, give it a few minutes and this will all be over." Serenity rubbed his cheek with the back of her hand. "How about I sing your favorite song?

Concentrate on the words and sing along with me in your head, okay?" Gideon's eyes shifted to hers.

Aaron listened as Serenity sang a song he'd known since he was a child, but with a few slight differences at the end.

"You are my sunshine,
My only sunshine.
You make me happy,
When skies are gray.
You never know dear,
How much I love you.
And that won't ever
Fade away."

Aaron's heart filled to the brim and expanded beyond what he thought was even possible. It wasn't the way Serenity looked at her son, or how much Gideon calmed while she sang. The woman had a beautiful voice. Did she have any idea how pretty and rich it was?

"All right, that's the worst part." The nurse put the needle on the tray. "Let's give it a couple of minutes, we'll get that cut all fixed up, and you can get out of here. You did a good job, slugger."

Serenity placed a kiss to his cheek. "I told you it'd be over quickly. You must have been singing really loudly in your head. I'm proud of you." She gave Aaron a shy smile. "I didn't like the original final line of the song. It made me sad. The whole song is. So I changed the chorus." She shrugged.

Aaron played the song over in his head to the original end of the song. *Please don't take my sunshine away.* "I can see that." He patted Gideon's hand. "You are doing awesome. I'm impressed you sing in your head. I bet you have as amazing a voice as your mom."

Aaron caught Serenity watching him. Emotions tumbled over themselves as they took turns dancing across her face. He wished they were somewhere else. Because right then, he'd tell her about how her singing voice wasn't the only thing that was amazing about her. She'd managed to get into his heart despite his attempts to keep the walls up. Now that he knew what life was like with her in it, he had no desire to go back to the way it was before.

Chapter Thirteen

Had Serenity heard that right? Aaron thought she had a beautiful voice? Compared to his, she found that hard to believe. A vague recollection of Mom and Grams complimenting her on it surfaced from the recesses of her mind. In the end, it didn't matter. As long as her voice helped Gideon relax like it had since he was a baby, it was all that mattered.

Until now. She suddenly wanted to know what else Aaron thought about her. Then again, if the intensity in his blue eyes was any indication, maybe it was better if she didn't. How was it possible that his presence made her calmer as she stood by her son's side, yet kicked her pulse into high gear at the same time?

As the nurse used five stitches to close the gash in her son's head, Serenity continued to sing to him. By the time it was finished, Gideon's eyelids were getting heavy and she could see sleep creeping in.

"I'll let them know you're taking the day off when I get back." Aaron looked at his watch. "I've got time.

Let me help you get him back to your house. Do you need any supplies?"

"No, I have a fully stocked first aid kit. Between Tuck and Lexi, they weren't going to leave me here without one." The stubborn part of her wanted to tell him she could get her son home all on her own. The practical side knew she would have accepted help from anyone of her family and it was silly to turn the offer down. She gave him what she hoped was a relieved smile. "I appreciate the help getting back. Something tells me he's going to be asleep by the time we get there."

"Of course."

The nurse came back with a care sheet and went over the instructions with Serenity. By the time they were given the go ahead to leave, she was more than ready to get out of there. She'd never liked hospitals, and even less when it was her son who was in one.

"Come on, big guy. Let's go." She scooped him into her arms and he snuggled his head under her chin. He was getting big and thinking about that made her sad. The idea that one day she wouldn't be able to carry him — or that he would be big enough to carry *her* — was something she refused to consider.

Aaron got to the door and then placed a hand on her back as she passed by. Thankful for his presence and help, she continued through the maze of hallways and out into the hot sun.

Once she was back behind the wheel of her car, she led the way to their duplex. Aaron held a hand out and she gave him her keys so he could unlock the door and open it for them. Before anyone could enter, Kia tried to dash out. Aaron picked up and held the kitten in his arms until he closed the door again.

Serenity set Gideon on the couch and retrieved his pillow and favorite blanket from his bedroom. He seemed happy to lie down and was asleep in moments. It didn't take long for Kia to settle at his feet.

Serenity used her fingers to gather her hair together and held it at the base of her neck. A forceful breath of air whooshed from her lungs and she leaned against the wall.

Aaron chuckled. "Are you going to be all right?"

"Yeah. It was my first ER visit with Gideon." She released the hair again and it cascaded down around her shoulders. "I suppose almost six years is pretty good, right?"

"I'd say so. And I never would have thought that — you handled it like a pro."

Serenity chuckled. She was glad to hear that. At least she didn't look like an insane mom. All she could do was her best. In the end, Gideon was home and sleeping peacefully. Her gaze rested on his bandage and she had to resist going over and kissing it. Feeling jittery, she shook her hands out.

Aaron must have noticed. "Why don't you get something to eat and drink? You haven't had lunch. You're probably starving."

Wow, she'd completely forgotten. "You're right." She led the way into the kitchen and opened the fridge. After getting the carton of orange juice, she poured herself a glass. "Would you like some?"

He shook his head. "I'm good, thanks. I need to get back to work here in a minute. I'll grab something on the way." The fridge was still open and he was studying the meager contents with a raised eyebrow. "I think you need to go grocery shopping."

Serenity put the glass of orange juice down without

taking a drink and nudged the fridge closed with a foot. "We're on a tight budget." She had no doubt any member of her family would have given her the same look if they saw the fridge, too. At the hospital, she hadn't given much thought to the medical bill that would inevitably come in the mail. Realizing it now made her want to curl up on the couch next to Gideon and pretend they didn't need anything from the real world. Not today. Her palms pressed against the surface of the table and she leaned forward.

"Hey, you." Aaron's strong hands grasped her arms and gently turned her to face him. "What is it?"

She made sure Gideon was still asleep and lowered her voice. "I have no idea how I'm going to pay the deductible from today." What was it about this man that seemed to coax the truth out of her? She was going to handle this. She had to. But the way he held her arms, looked at her with compassion, made her want to lean into him. Share the burden. But it wasn't his responsibility.

~

Aaron could see the war waging inside Serenity. Her gaze flitted from his face to something behind him. She was fighting it — battling against letting him into her life.

"Things'll come together. Your family will…"

"No." She shook her head. "I've let people bail me out of situations all my life. I can't let them do it again." She looked desperate.

"You couldn't be more wrong." His hands slid up her arms to frame her face. "You could have bailed out of motherhood, but you didn't. You chose to raise

Gideon and love him no matter what. When you moved here, you weren't bailing. You were doing the exact opposite. You left behind your support system to start a new life. You didn't bail today when your son needed you most. In fact, you held it together for him when I bet you felt like you were falling apart inside." *God, please let her see the truth in this.*

Tears filled her eyes and she tried to blink them away. The warmth from her cheeks sent sensations skittering across his skin. A lone tear escaped and slid down the side of her face. Aaron used the pad of his thumb to wipe it away.

"You, Serenity Chandler, are a strong woman who is doing what she needs to for her family. You can handle anything on your own. But it doesn't mean you should."

She took in a deep breath and released it. The vulnerability on her face hit him right in the gut, but it was the trust in her eyes that pierced his heart. There were many reasons why he should take a step back and leave. But all of them — including his job — shrank in comparison to the possibilities that could exist with the woman standing in front of him. If he left now, he knew he'd regret not giving this a chance.

Against his better judgement, he threaded his fingers through the silky strands of her hair. His fingertips brushed the skin on the back of her neck.

Completely lost in the depth of her chocolate eyes, he heard her inhale sharply when she lifted a hand and lightly stroked the hair that was curling over his ears. Her fingers were soft and cool against his skin. They were close enough now that her warm breath touched his chin.

Aaron moved, his lips lightly brushing hers. She

leaned into him and he put an arm around her waist, bringing her closer. He dipped his head and explored her lips in a gentle caress. He hoped it expressed not only his interest in her but his need to be there for her — to be the person she could count on.

When she clasped her hands behind his neck and murmured his name, his heart leapt in his chest. He wanted to continue kissing her, to hold her forever. If only that were possible.

He rested his forehead against hers and took a fortifying breath. "I've got to get back to work. I'm sorry." Leaving was the last thing he wanted to do. In a matter of minutes, everything in his life had changed. He was going to talk to Cynthia, go to the board. There had to be something he could do about the guidelines and he wasn't going to give up until he found a way around them.

Serenity lifted her chin. "I know. I understand. Thank you for coming with us to the hospital."

"You're welcome. Can I call later and see how you're both doing?" She nodded, pulling her bottom lip in between her teeth. Aaron groaned and captured that lip in a brief kiss. Heaven help him, it was going to take a train to drag him away from her if he didn't move now. He took a step backwards but kept holding her hands in his. "I'll call you tonight. Try to get some rest while Gideon's sleeping. Tell him I'm thinking about him, okay?"

"I will."

They stared at each other until Aaron chuckled and kissed her cheek. "Okay. I'm leaving now."

She giggled. "Bye, Aaron."

"Bye, Serenity."

He heard the door click closed behind him and took

the stairs two at a time. His mind was already going over options and plans for how he could pursue a relationship with Serenity and still keep his job. There had to be a way because walking away from the beautiful woman and her son was no longer an option.

~

Serenity's hand lingered on the doorknob. She softly touched a finger to her lips and smiled. The scent of Aaron's woodsy aftershave lingered in the air. She took in a deep breath as the memory of being in his arms enveloped her.

Gideon shifted on the couch and she turned to check on him. His eyes remained closed, his mouth open slightly as he slept. She brushed some hair away from his face before going back to the kitchen and sitting down.

Her phone buzzed and she picked it up to see who the text was from. Aaron's name flashed on the screen.

"Let me know if you guys need me to bring anything by tonight. I miss you already."

She grinned and texted him back.

"Thanks. I think we'll be fine. I miss you, too."

Nervous energy collided with a giddiness that drove Serenity from her chair to the sink. She might as well wash the dishes because she wasn't going to be able to concentrate on much else for a long while.

~

Aaron arrived back at the school. He whistled as he made his way down the hall and ran into Zane.

His friend raised an eyebrow and grinned. "You'd

better not let Cynthia catch you this happy after spending time with Serenity."

"What are you even talking about?"

"You're whistling and all dreamy-eyed. You remind me of a love-sick teenager."

Aaron shifted his weight under Zane's scrutiny as heat climbed the back of his neck. He shrugged, admitting defeat on this one. They continued down the hallway to Aaron's classroom.

"I'm not saying you did anything wrong. But Cynthia heard about the injury and someone mentioned you'd gone to check on them. Word is, she didn't look too thrilled."

Yeah, because that was unusual. Aaron wasn't sure he'd ever seen her look anything but unhappy. Even still, if she so much as suspected he had feelings for Serenity, his job could be on the line. Serenity's, too, if Cynthia decided to get nasty. They were going to have to keep it behind the scenes at work until he could arrange a meeting with the board.

Aaron moved to close the door to his classroom. "She's been in a bad mood all day."

Zane crossed his arms and sat on the corner of a table. "How's Gideon doing? Letty's texted me twice asking if I'd heard from you."

"He's okay. Serenity took him home. He ended up with five stitches and was a real champ the whole time. I imagine Serenity will wait and see how he is tomorrow to decide whether he'll be coming back to school then or needs a day."

Zane withdrew his cell phone and typed out a text message. Aaron assumed he was filling Letty in. "I'm glad he's okay. She was shaken up about it. She hates it when a student gets hurt on her watch."

Aaron smiled. "That's because she's one of the best teachers I've known. These kids are lucky to have her. I'm planning on calling Serenity this evening. I'll be sure to text you when I get an update on Gideon."

"Thanks." Zane studied him for a moment and grinned. "You're falling for Serenity, aren't you?"

"Am I that obvious?"

Zane shrugged. "Maybe just to those who know you well. What are you going to do, man?"

Aaron groaned and pinched the bridge of his nose. "I'm working on a plan to approach the board and officially request that the guideline be dropped." He wished he felt certain about the plan actually working. "Serenity's never mentioned the guidelines. I'm not sure she even knows about them. It's only fair that I talk to her about it — give her a heads-up." Thinking about the conversation filled him with dread. What if she thought it was enough of a reason to put an end to their relationship before it had a chance to start? "Especially if there's a chance Cynthia could get nasty about it and fire us both. I'm pretty sure losing her job would mean Gideon leaving the school. I can't be responsible for that."

Zane shook his head. "You're getting way ahead of yourself."

"I don't think I am."

Zane nodded. "You know you have our support. If there's anything we can do to help, let us know."

"I appreciate that." He watched as Zane went through the door and disappeared from sight. Despite the worry over what he should do about Cynthia, the memory of his kiss with Serenity kept his heart sailing the rest of the afternoon.

Chapter Fourteen

It'd been over twenty-four hours since Serenity had watched Aaron walk out her door and it felt more like an eternity. The feel of his lips on hers left an impression that wasn't going to fade anytime soon. She hadn't let a man get close to her since Jay. She'd never even been tempted. Yet she managed to meet a man that had the ability to send her heart galloping with one of his smiles.

Not unlike his toe-curling kisses. Her hand moved to touch her lips of their own accord. Memories of the way he'd held her brought color to her cheeks and warmth to her heart.

She'd felt safe. Wanted.

And it scared her. Ever since she and Gideon moved, she'd been handling everything on her own. It was exactly what she wanted to do. Except that Aaron made her want to lean on him.

True to his word, Aaron had called last night after he got home. They talked about work, the weather, Serenity's crochet, and Aaron's music. Before she knew it, the clock read eleven and they decided they should probably say goodbye and get some rest.

Before hanging up the phone, Aaron had asked if he could bring pizza by the next day and have an early dinner with them. Serenity wasn't about to turn him down.

Now she kept pacing between the kitchen and the living room, as if that would move time along any quicker. She made another batch of cookies and had them cooling on the counter. She'd taken one to Gideon in his room when she heard something at the front door.

Blood raced through her veins as she forced herself to walk calmly to the door. She pulled it open, a smile already stretching across her face.

To find no one outside.

Gideon raced up beside her and she stuck a hand out to stop him from exiting the house. "Hold on, big guy. I thought that was the Music Man. But no one's here. Stay inside for a minute, please." She waited long enough to make sure he obeyed and took several steps out onto the porch. She swiveled her head, taking in the front of the house and street.

There was nothing worth being alarmed about, but the hair on the back of her neck stood on end. Kia rubbed against her ankles. Serenity picked her up and absently rubbed her ears.

Serenity shivered just as Aaron's car parked along the curb. He got out and jogged around the vehicle to the passenger side where he retrieved three pizza boxes. A bright smile lit up his face until he got close enough to see her expression. Concern flashed in his eyes. "What's wrong?"

She told him about the sound at the door, chill bumps lining her arms. She didn't feel as exposed now that Aaron was there, but she still couldn't quite shake the impression that they were being watched. With a wary glance at the road, she started to close the door behind them.

Aaron shot her a concerned glance and set the boxes down on the table. "I'm going to go outside and take a look."

Serenity shook her head. "I'm sure I'm being paranoid."

He appeared doubtful. "I'm a fan of listening to your instincts. I'll be right back."

She stayed at the door until he returned. "Did you see anything?"

"Nothing obvious. You're keeping your doors locked at all times, right?"

She nodded and closed the door. She set Kia down on the floor. "I'm almost neurotic about it."

"Good. If you see anyone snooping around, let me know."

"Thank you."

Aaron lightly touched her arm. "You're welcome." He reacted quickly as Gideon flew through the air and into his arms. "Hey! You seem to be feeling better today. How's your head?"

Gideon put a hand on the bandage and smiled before going back to the dominoes he was lining up on the kitchen floor.

"He hasn't complained of any pain. He's a tough kid." Serenity retrieved the plates and napkins from the counter and set them beside the pizza. "If it weren't for the gauze, you'd have never known anything happened." She headed back for the kitchen to retrieve glasses of water.

"I'm glad to hear that." Aaron caught her arm on

the way by, gently tugging her to a stop in front of him. "I'm glad we're having dinner together. I see you every other day of the week and find I miss you a great deal on Saturdays."

Serenity smiled as his words warmed her. "I know exactly what you mean." The man had been there less than ten minutes and she already wanted to feel his arms around her again. Good grief, they hadn't even eaten yet.

Aaron released her arm and motioned towards the boxes. "I brought two kinds of pizza plus breadsticks. I wasn't sure what you guys preferred, so I went with the basics."

Serenity lifted the lids and took in a whiff. "Pepperoni and sausage. You can't go wrong with that." She got the glasses of water. "I haven't had pizza in a while — which is sad, really."

The aroma must have made its way into the rest of the house because Gideon followed it out to the table and took his seat. Aaron prayed for their food and as soon as "Amen" had been uttered, Gideon took a giant bite of his breadstick with gusto. He ate half of it before even looking at the small slice of pizza in front of him.

Serenity chuckled. "It's like you read his mind. He loves breadsticks. He rarely eats pizza, but I always offer just in case. You know, when he was a toddler, he ate pepperoni pizza. Then he'd only eat it if it were cheese. Now even that's rare." The variety of foods her son ate seemed to decrease all the time and it worried her. She tried to focus on the things he did eat and be thankful for that. She'd heard of kids with autism who ate much less than he did. It could be worse.

She caught Aaron watching her and realized she

must have had a faraway look on her face. She gave him a reassuring smile and held up her slice of pepperoni. "But no worries, I'll make up for him." She raised an eyebrow and took a bite. The melted cheese stretched from her mouth to the pizza and she had to use the other hand to break it off before it became more embarrassing than it already was.

His lips stretched into a wide grin before he took a bite of his own, facing the same problem she had. They were both laughing by the time they'd finished their mouthfuls. Gideon watched them. The expression on his face told them he didn't get it at all, which made them laugh harder.

Serenity enjoyed the meal immensely. Her eyes widened at the amount of food that remained. "I think you could have brought half this and it would've been plenty."

"If I did that, there wouldn't have been any leftovers for you." He winked.

The nearly empty fridge yesterday must have made an impression on him. Normally, she would have been embarrassed at the possibility that he thought he needed to bring them food so they'd have enough to eat. But the look in his eyes reassured her he was only being kind. "I appreciate the thought. Thank you."

"You're welcome." He motioned to the boxes. "Do you think Gideon will want more?"

"I doubt it. I'll leave the food on his plate out a little while longer in case he changes his mind."

Her son had gone back to building with dominoes.

Aaron gathered the food and put it in the fridge for her. Serenity cleaned off the table and tossed the cloth into the sink from the doorway.

"Nice shot." Aaron's voice was low as he bent to

place a kiss on her cheek. He squeezed her hand before moving to sit on the floor near Gideon.

She listened to his deep voice as he commented on the domino setup. She sat down on the futon to check e-mail on her phone. Gideon must have sent the dominoes falling because after the loud clatter, both guys clapped enthusiastically.

Aaron was still smiling when he walked into the living room. "He's got skill for creating some of those taller structures. Who knows, maybe he'll become an architect when he grows up."

Serenity could picture that. Gideon liked to work with his hands and create things.

Aaron paused by the futon and motioned to the cushion next to her. "Is this spot free?"

"It is." Serenity tried to focus on something else to keep the rush of color from her face. The futon dipped as he settled next to her, his arm close enough to brush against hers.

~

Aaron felt the warmth of her arm against his. He reached for her hand, enjoying the way it seemed to disappear in his own. Her fingers were long and delicate. They'd be perfect for playing the piano. His mind searched for a conversation starter to keep his thoughts from focusing on how badly he wanted to kiss her again. "Did you two have a relaxing day?"

"We did. We watched a movie earlier. He's been happy to sit around and play. Sometimes our weeks are so busy we have to decompress over the weekend. Hey, did you hear whether they got the printer fixed yesterday?"

"Yes, it's working normally now. Although I heard Cynthia complained the whole time the repairman was there."

"Thank goodness. I was dreading going into work on Monday if they hadn't."

Monday. Aaron thought about his schedule for the new week and scowled. "I'm not going to be here for lunch that day. My mother's going to be in town. She's never here long and wants me to meet her for lunch. I didn't want you to think I forgot and blew it off."

"Thanks for letting me know. I hope the visit with your mom goes well."

Aaron stifled a groan. "Yeah, so do I. But usually, when she comes to visit, there's some ulterior motive behind it. And as a side bonus, I get to hear complaints about the latest man in her life."

"That sounds stressful. What brought her to town?"

He absently rubbed the top of her thumb with his own. He pictured the small graveyard nestled in the trees about a half hour's drive away. The marker with his brother's name on it was in a section of the graveyard where the area was covered with bluebonnets in the spring. During the summer, lush green grass grew around it. *Beloved son and brother.* He shook to clear the engraved words from his mind.

Serenity was watching him when he looked up, chewing on her lip and concern drawing her brows together. She gave his hand a squeeze.

He took a settling breath. "Today is my little brother's birthday. She always comes to town long enough to visit his grave." Irritation rose like bile in his throat. "My father comes around in the evening. Because they can't stand to be in the same place at the same time. I'll meet him for dinner." Aaron rarely spoke about his family, so why was he suddenly sharing all of this with Serenity?

Maybe it was because she was watching him with eyes that held the right balance of understanding and concern. What he appreciated was the lack of pity. The last thing he wanted was to be pitied for what his parents did — or didn't do. But saying it aloud was easing some of the pressure that'd been pushing in on his chest all day. He dreaded this date all year. Even though he thought about Kenneth often, most of his favorite memories revolved around Christmas. That's when he went to visit his brother's grave, leaving a new toy zebra — Kenneth's favorite.

"If they can't keep things civil for an hour to meet in your brother's memory, they're putting themselves first. And no one wins."

Aaron's eyebrows flew up at her quick assessment of his family's dynamics. She was hitting it dead on. "You're not wrong."

They were silent for a minute or two until Serenity cleared her throat. "What happened to your brother?"

He knew that question was coming. It was completely natural to wonder. He hated having to answer it. But this time, for some reason, the normal barbs of pain and resentment the memory brought to the surface seemed a bit duller with her there. Aaron pushed that realization down, unwilling to explore it. Not now.

A quick glance assured him Gideon wasn't in the room. He released Serenity's hand and ran fingers through his hair. "Kenneth was four years younger than I was. He had autism and while he was verbal, he was also prone to wandering."

Serenity pulled her knees to her chest and rested her

chin on them. Her cocoa eyes stayed on him and he continued.

"My parents were usually good about making sure doors were secured so he couldn't get out of the house." He swallowed the lump of emotions that threatened to lodge themselves in his throat. "When he was six, we were getting ready to sit down and eat dinner. But we couldn't find Kenneth anywhere. We found the back door unlocked and hanging open. They called the police and there was a frantic search for him."

Serenity's feet fell to the floor and she covered her mouth with her hands, her eyes wide and shining with tears. "Oh, Aaron."

"They found him an hour later in the neighbor's pool. There was nothing they could do." Despite every attempt to maintain control over his emotions, there was still a catch in his voice. "My parents spent the next two years blaming each other and keeping me so busy with after school activities that I only went home to sleep." He pinched the bridge of his nose and ran a hand down the side of his face. "This is going to sound horrible, but it was a relief when they finally divorced. And even more so when I turned eighteen and could move out on my own."

His eyes flitted from a spot on the coffee table to Serenity's face. She brushed a tear away and sniffed. "I can't even imagine going through what you have. I'm sorry you experienced that." She sniffed again. "Your brother must have been an amazing kid. What was he like?"

Aaron thought about Kenneth, all of the fun memories coming to the surface. A smile brought the corners of his mouth upwards in spite of the mix of emotions vying for attention. "Kenneth was smart. He could read novels at the age of five. He loved zebras more than anything and he knew everything there was to know about them." Aaron chuckled. "He'd spend an hour or more telling me about the different facts he'd learned. One time, Mom took us to the zoo and we never made it past the zebra enclosure."

Serenity was smiling too. She shifted on the couch until she was facing him, her legs crossed in front of her. Dark hair flowed down past her shoulders to almost touch the cushion she sat on. "That's awesome. I'll bet it drove you crazy sometimes."

"Definitely. We didn't have a lot in common, but we sang together. We even made up songs about zebras." He laughed again. "I decided to become a music therapist because of him. It always made him happy and I grew up wanting to help other kids in a similar way."

"I know you're making a difference in Gideon's life. And every other student that steps a foot into your classroom." Serenity gave him a watery smile. "Kenneth would be proud of you."

"Thank you." Aaron reached for her hand again in hopes of hiding the warmth he felt creeping up the back of his neck. Even when he'd told Zane about Kenneth, he'd kept the details vague. If someone had told him he'd spill his guts to Serenity even a few days ago, he would have said they were crazy. Now, he was glad he had. The heavy weight on his shoulders eased a bit.

Aaron turned her hand over and laid it on his knee. With his other hand, he caressed the skin on the underside of her wrist. It was as smooth as satin and he was tempted to touch his lips to it.

Gideon ran in, tossing a train onto Serenity's lap. She gave Aaron's hand a small squeeze and let go to fix the wheel that had come off the engine. Once it was good to go, Gideon retrieved a collection of train cars and brought them back, setting them up on the living room floor.

Aaron stayed at the house another hour before he decided to head home. Serenity walked him to the door. Aaron waved to Gideon behind her before turning his full attention to the woman standing in front of him. "I'll see you tomorrow at church."

She nodded. "Thanks again for the pizza. It was great."

"You're welcome."

Gideon stood next to his mom, his arms wrapped around hers.

Aaron desperately wanted to pull Serenity to him and kiss her like they had the day before. But he couldn't, not with her son watching them. Serenity gave him a grin that was a cross between sympathetic and humorous. He chuckled, gave up, and placed a kiss on her cheek near her ear. "Bye."

"Goodbye." She gave him a little wave before closing the door behind him.

Aaron took in a fortifying breath as he got into his car. He didn't need any more incentive to find a way around the policy at work. But if he had, there was no doubt about it. Serenity had completely embedded herself in his heart.

Chapter Fifteen

It was just as well that she wasn't supposed to meet Aaron for lunch. Serenity would've had to cancel on him, anyway. She'd walked into work that morning with a note waiting for her on the desk:

Serenity,
Please come see me at 1 p.m. today. I have something I wish to speak with you about. Thank you.
Cynthia

She'd dreaded the meeting all morning. Maggie was kind enough to trade lunch hours with her so at least Serenity was able to eat beforehand. It had been odd eating lunch at the same time as the majority of the other people at the school. Serenity even saw Letty and Zane for a short while.

She said a prayer that things were going well for Aaron and his mom. They'd talked about the whole thing more on the phone and he promised he'd call her tonight to tell her about it and the dinner with his dad. She'd made him promise, even if it was late when he got home again.

On her way to Cynthia's office, Serenity tried to quell the ball of nerves bouncing around in her stomach. She didn't know the woman and, while she tended to be a little demanding, hadn't had any horrible experiences to set her on edge. But she'd heard enough from her co-workers to know that Cynthia didn't call people in to pay them a compliment.

She paused at her door for a deep breath and knocked. Cynthia's voice summoned her inside.

The office was decorated with every kind of flower Serenity could imagine. From photos on the walls to the sun catcher in the lone window, to the pot of pen flowers on her desk. Serenity blinked against the assault of color. She hadn't known what to expect from Cynthia's office, but the cheeriness was not something she would've bet on.

"Thank you for coming by, Serenity. Please have a seat."

Serenity eased into the chair opposite Cynthia. It was much lower than she anticipated. In fact, the other woman seated at her desk chair seemed significantly taller and Serenity could only assume the differences were intentional.

This was not a good sign of the conversation to come.

Cynthia cleared her throat. "I heard that your son was injured on the playground Friday. How is he doing?"

Was that all she wanted to talk about? Maybe this wouldn't be bad after all. "He's healing up fine, thank you. He's back to school today and if you didn't see the bandage on his head, you'd never know he hit it." She smiled.

"Good. Good. I'm glad to hear that." Cynthia shuffled some papers around on her desk. Once she'd finished, the expression on her face turned to something much more serious. "When you began working here, there was a packet of guidelines and school rules that you should have been given. Did you receive that information?"

Serenity thought back to her hiring process. She didn't remember getting anything then, but they had received a booklet with school policies when Gideon enrolled. She told Cynthia as much. Her mind flew through what she could remember, trying to figure out which one of them she might have violated.

"I understand that our music therapist, Aaron Randall, accompanied you to the hospital."

"Yes. He helped me get Gideon there and then back home again afterwards." What did Aaron have to do with any of this?

"I see. That was thoughtful of him." Her expression didn't relay the same sentiment. She studied Serenity over the tips of her fingers that she kept steepled in front of her nose. "I've also heard that the two of you eat lunch together most of the time. Is that correct?"

"Yes. We both usually take a late lunch. I met him in the breakroom the week I started working here."

Cynthia gave a definitive nod. She slid a piece of paper across the desk. "I want to make sure that you saw this particular guideline. I wouldn't want you or Aaron to run into any complications because of it."

Completely confused, Serenity's eyes moved from Cynthia's face to the paper and scanned it. Then she went through and read it in detail. Nausea rolled through her gut as the words sank in. She definitely had not been made aware of the policy before today. "Can

I keep this copy?"

"Of course." Cynthia waved her away. "If you have any questions about it, I hope you know you can come to me."

Serenity nodded, numb. She said her farewell and left the office quickly. As soon as she got back to her desk, she had Maggie's full attention.

"What did she want?"

Serenity held up the paper. "Apparently, I was unaware of one of the guidelines and since Aaron and I have been spending some extra time together, she thought it was prudent I did." Her words dripped with sarcasm as her mind raced. Was Aaron aware of the policy? If so, why hadn't he warned her? From the wording, it sounded like he was putting his job at risk if they pursued anything more than friendship. Could she be fired, too?

Maggie looked sad. "I'm sorry. The whole thing's a mess. Did you hear what happened at the end of the last school year?"

Serenity shook her head.

Maggie told her about the administrator who had started seeing one of the student's moms and how the whole thing had blown up in the middle of the hallway. "I guess Cynthia has decided something like that isn't going to happen again."

"Doesn't that seem a bit extreme, though? If situations like that came up every school year, then that might be different."

"I agree." Maggie shrugged. "But the board of directors voted the policy through. There's not a lot the rest of us can do about it." She studied Serenity. "I hate to see it get in the way of a good thing." She lowered her voice. "You and the Music Man have chemistry.

Everyone can see it."

Fantastic. She needed to stay off the radar and if everyone could tell that there was something possibly going on between them now, well, that wasn't a good thing. Her chest tight, she went through the motions for the rest of the day, eager to escape the confines of the school.

~

Aaron flopped onto the couch, a loud groan escaping as he stretched out. He'd been on his feet most of the day and the few times he had been able to sit down — primarily at meals — the conversation was emotionally taxing enough to add to his exhaustion.

It was almost ten and he hesitated to call Serenity. But she'd made him promise. He caught a glimpse of her twice while at work and even managed to wave once, but hearing her voice would be the highlight.

"Hey, Music Man. Did you survive the day?"

The sound of her voice, lovely and melodic, flowed over him.

"Barely. I'm glad to be home again." He laid an arm over his eyes, blocking out the light fixture above him. "It could have been worse. They were both on their best behavior. And now that's done for another year."

It sounded like Serenity took a drink of something. "Do you see them any other time of the year?"

He shrugged, even though she couldn't possibly see the movement. "A Christmas here and there, but not normally. I'm okay with that." She was silent for a few moments. "Are you still there?"

A sigh came over the receiver. "Yeah. I'm sorry. I guess I'm just dragging tonight."

"Did your day go all right?" There was no answer. "Serenity?"

"Everything went fine. Gideon had a great day at school and Letty told me he never complained about his head."

"That's good to hear. When do his stitches come out again?"

"A week from today. But my Grams' birthday party is Sunday and we're going to Kitner for the weekend. My sister will probably remove them for us."

"I didn't realize you were going back home. That'll be nice for you to get to see everyone."

"I'm looking forward to it. The Chandler get-togethers are always interesting." Humor colored her voice.

Aaron imagined the way her lips tilted up at the corners when she smiled. Was she lounging on her couch like him? Or was she sitting at her kitchen table? Right now, he wished he could reach out and hold her hand. "It sounds like fun. I'll miss you."

She paused. "I should probably go. Gideon was up several times last night. If he does that again …"

He couldn't put his finger on it, but there was something in her voice. If she'd been up so much with Gideon, hopefully she was just tired. "You don't have to say another word. Get some rest. I'll see you tomorrow?"

"Tomorrow."

They said goodnight and he hung up the phone.

The next morning, he went to work thankful for a normal day. All morning, he counted down the hours until lunch. Serenity greeted him at their table with a bright smile, but it didn't take long to realize the hesitation he felt last night was still there.

She seemed less talkative. And when he asked if she was all right, she insisted she was. But her gaze remained fixed on her food or other activity in the breakroom.

By the time lunch was over, Aaron's gut told him something was going on and clearly Serenity wasn't going to talk about it at work.

A knock at his classroom brought his attention to Zane. "I have a moment and wanted to give you a heads-up."

"Oh?"

Zane came into the room and rolled his shoulders before leaning against the wall. "Cynthia summoned Serenity to her office yesterday. Word has it she made sure Serenity read the new policy. Then Cynthia quizzed her on why you went to the ER Friday."

Aaron groaned, sinking to the corner of his desk. No doubt that was what caused her to be so standoffish today.

"You never discussed the guidelines?"

Aaron shook his head. "I kept meaning to, but things didn't really go beyond a friendship level until Friday." He kicked at the chair leg. Stupid! If she hadn't known about them, did she think he was trying to hide them from her? "I meant to bring them up over the weekend and didn't." That was going to come back to haunt him.

"Don't overthink it yet, man. Go see her tonight and talk to her then. The sooner you guys get it all out in the open, the better it'll be for both of you."

Aaron knew that was true. He nodded. "I'll text her and see if I can do that." He pushed away from the desk. "The last thing I want to do is mess this up."

"Letty and I will be praying."

"I appreciate that."

When Zane left, Aaron texted Serenity. "Can I come by tonight and talk?"

Twenty long minutes later, he got her response. "Okay. See you then."

It was going to take a miracle for Aaron to focus on anything but the upcoming conversation for the rest of the workday.

Chapter Sixteen

Despite her best attempts to stay busy, Serenity continuously paced back and forth across the living room. Aaron should be here any moment now. What did he want to talk about? Something told her it was the same topic that had been haunting her the last day or so.

A knock at the door made her jump. She strode across the room and unlocked it. She pulled it open, ushering Aaron inside.

"Hey."

"Hi." He slipped his hands into his pockets. His eyes focused on her face and it looked like he was trying to decide what to say.

"Do you want to sit down?" Serenity led the way to the couch. "What did you want to talk about?"

Aaron absently scratched his jaw. "I heard Cynthia called you into her office yesterday."

Serenity nodded. "Did you know about the new policy?"

"I did."

"And you didn't think it prudent to tell me before we — before whatever this is — started?" Serenity crossed her arms over her chest. "At the very least, you're risking your job."

He inhaled deeply and reached across the space between them to place a hand on her arm. The touch sent shivers up and down her spine.

"For one thing, I assumed they went over the policies with you when they hired you. Cynthia's been on a crusade with the dating one specifically. I'm surprised she didn't sit you down and explain it in detail before you started work." He slid his hand down to hers and squeezed it. "I didn't expect any of this to happen."

Serenity focused on the warmth of his hand. "Neither did I." She sighed. "I was given a large number of papers at my interview and I looked through them all one evening, but if I saw those guidelines, they didn't stick out in my mind." His expression was serious and worry gnawed at her stomach. "Maggie told me a little about why Cynthia insisted on changing the guidelines. It seems overboard."

"I agree. But Cynthia has made it her personal goal to stop something similar from happening again."

"And one person can do that?"

"Yeah. She's got the blessing of the rest of the board of directors." Aaron's thumb lightly rubbed the skin on her palm. "The whole thing is still new. We haven't seen whether she'll move forward with the consequences or if it's all a bunch of hot air."

Gideon wandered through the room to the kitchen. Serenity leaned against the back of the couch and moved her hand from Aaron's. She listened as Gideon opened the refrigerator door and took out his partial cup of chocolate milk from earlier in the day. He clutched it in his hands as he re-entered the living room. "Hey, big guy. Leave the cup on the table so it doesn't spill in your room." He took another swig before doing as she asked. After that, he bounded back down the hall. Serenity sighed, returning to their previous conversation. "Does the fact that we both work there change anything?"

"I doubt it. You're the mother of one of my students. I think that's all that matters to Cynthia." Aaron ran a hand through his hair. "It wasn't a big deal when we were just friends. But now…" His blue eyes studied her face, waiting for her response.

"You mean the fact that you're here at my house means we're at risk of losing our jobs?" Seriously? It sounded like something from a bad reality television show. "Aaron, I can't afford to lose my job. Everything from this house to Gideon's education hinges on it."

"Cynthia's concerned about maintaining a professional environment at the Academy. What we do on our own time — as long as it stays out of work — should be okay. It ought to be."

Serenity shook her head. "I agree that it should. But if she's making inquiries now …" They'd barely started a relationship, but the thought of it ending left her with a wave of sadness. "I'm not sure I can risk it. I need this job." She dropped her voice. "And I've got the bill from the ER visit coming. I'm not sure how I'm going to pay it now, much less if I become unemployed."

"I do understand. Our situations are different, but my job and those kids I teach are important to me. I don't want to get fired, either. But I could find another job." He paused, his blue eyes boring straight into hers.

"I'll never find someone else like you."

Serenity's breathing sped up as she processed his words. No other man had been able to affect her like this before. He made her want to think about forever, no matter how dangerous that might be. "But what can we do?"

He curled one hand into a fist and bounced it off his knee. "Cynthia's response to the mess earlier this year is overkill and I still can't believe the rest of the board of directors went with it. Maybe I can go to someone else on the board and speak with them."

"And what if they hear the reason you want to change the guidelines and fire us both on the spot?" Serenity wanted to believe there was a way out. But entertaining the risk they'd be taking made her doubt everything.

Aaron shifted on the couch so that his right knee touched her left. "I wish I had a good answer." He remained silent in thought for a short time before turning his body towards her. "I want you to know that *this* — between us — I want us to have the chance to see where it leads."

Serenity's eyes slid shut and anguish stabbed at her heart. "So do I. But I also have to put Gideon first." She opened them again. "I'm sorry."

Pain flitted across Aaron's face and he slumped against the back of the couch. "Can we at least be friends? I don't want to lose you completely."

Aaron was the first person she'd gotten close to outside of her family. But could she go back to being just friends with him? The painful beat of her heart said she wasn't so sure. Especially when all she needed at that moment was for him to hold her close. "I don't want that, either." Tears were building and she would not cry in front of him. She refused.

Aaron studied her closely. Was he questioning her words? Or could he tell how miserable she was? "I'm sorry, Serenity."

She nodded, fixing her eyes on the floor. If she looked at him now, she was going to cry. He put a finger under her chin and lifted it until her eyes focused on him.

"I'm going to be praying we figure a way out of this. We'll take a big step back, but promise me you won't give up on us completely."

A single tear escaped, slowly sliding its way down her cheek. He swiped it away with his thumb and she nodded her agreement.

Aaron stood, placed a kiss to her wet cheek, and left. When the front door clicked shut, she slid the deadbolt into place. Only then did she allow herself to lean against it and let the tears flow freely.

~

Aaron's week was proving to be the longest he could remember experiencing — and it was only Thursday. No matter what he tried to focus his mind on, he kept picturing the way Serenity had looked the other night before he left her house.

On his way over there, he'd played through every possible scenario, hoping for the best. Even though he'd half expected it, hearing Serenity say she wanted them to go back to being friends had been one of the worst things that could have happened.

At least she was still in his life. Not in the way he wanted, but it was better than losing her completely.

She'd promised she wouldn't give up on them.

Neither would he.

He was going to find a way to make this work. For now, though, getting through the week was going to take a miracle.

Aaron needed to make some copies so he took a deep breath and purposefully strode through the school to the main office. Seeing Serenity sitting at the desk with Maggie made his stomach do a flip flop. He didn't think she'd spotted him yet.

Maggie gave a plate a shove, the cookies piled on it shifting as they sailed across the desk to Serenity. "One of the parents left this for us today. I thought that was sweet." Maggie motioned for Aaron to join them. "We've got plenty, help yourself."

Serenity's eyes widened. She picked the plate up and held it out to him. He reached for a cookie and took a bite. He'd expected the usual chocolate. "Oatmeal raisin. One of my favorites."

"Really?" Serenity took a nibble of her own cookie. "Mine, too. I'm the only one in my family who likes them so I don't get to eat them very often."

Maggie chuckled and waved her long fingernails at them, making the cats painted on them appear to dance. "You two fight over them then. Why anyone would choose to eat a raisin cookie over chocolate chip is beyond me."

Aaron's heart stuttered when Serenity's gaze darted from his face to something on her desk. She licked away a crumb that was on her lip.

They'd managed to avoid each other most of the week. The one lunch they had eaten together included another person, which turned out to be a blessing if the lack of conversation was any indication.

It'd taken all of Aaron's willpower to not text or call

her. He'd made sure to ask about Gideon, but otherwise, they'd hardly spoken. He missed it desperately.

Aaron snagged one more cookie and gave Serenity a wink. "The rest are all yours." He strode over to the copy machine and went to work. Even though his back was turned to the ladies at the front desk, Maggie's voice could easily be heard over the whir of the copier as she talked to Serenity.

"What are your plans for the weekend?"

"Gideon and I are going to Kitner for my Grams' eighty-seventh birthday party." Aaron could hear the smile in her voice. "We're going to stay there Saturday night and come home Sunday afternoon."

Aaron glanced at her. He had forgotten about her trip to Kitner. It would mean he wouldn't see her in church on Sunday. His disappointment was keen, but he knew that the break was something she probably really needed.

Maggie adjusted the thick-rimmed glasses that sat on her nose. Aaron guessed that they served no purpose except for assisting in her fashion statement. "How fun! My Nanna turned eighty last month. She's the one who raised me. There's nothing like a grandmother, huh?"

"Amen to that."

Letty hurried in, a stack of papers in her arms. She stopped in front of Serenity and blew some strands of hair out of her eyes. "Hey! The guys at the church are getting together for a basketball game Tuesday night. I and a bunch of the other ladies often go to visit and sometimes throw verbal jabs at the men." She grinned. "Do you want to join us?"

Aaron was going to be playing in that friendly game

of ball. He couldn't hide his interest as he turned around to see Serenity's response.

She hesitated, her eyes going from Letty to him and then back again. Aaron suspected she was trying to think of a way to get out of going. Apparently, she couldn't find a good enough reason. She finally nodded. "That sounds like fun. We'll plan on coming."

"Great!" Letty seemed genuinely pleased. "I've got to run, one of my aides is watching the class. I forgot these in my office this morning." She rolled her eyes. "I'll talk to you later."

Aaron finished his copies and escaped the office. Despite the busy afternoon, all he could think about was the fact that Serenity would be watching him play basketball on Tuesday. He'd text Zane later and see if he was up to getting in a practice between now and then.

Chapter Seventeen

Serenity and Gideon arrived at the Chandler house right before noon on Saturday. She'd expected to spend the day with them until Grams' party that evening, but Mom insisted she go out and get the haircut she'd been talking about while they watched Gideon.

By the time she got back to the house, she wondered why she hadn't had it cut sooner. Now that her hair was nearly thirteen inches shorter, it felt like her head was floating without all of that weight. Serenity chuckled when she realized she'd have to use about a third less shampoo when she washed it, too.

She discovered everyone in the living room when she walked into the house. Gideon immediately approached her, his face serious.

"What do you think, big guy? Do you like it?"

Gideon ran his fingers through her hair several times and then cupped the ends in both hands, bouncing them.

Serenity laughed. "I know! It feels funny, doesn't

it?"

Gideon smiled, ran his fingers through her hair one last time, and went to play.

Mom tucked some of Serenity's hair behind her ear and gave a satisfied nod. "I guess he gave it the official seal of approval. I have to agree. It looks lovely, sweetheart."

"Thanks, Mom." Serenity beamed.

"It is pretty." Grams patted the spot on the couch next to her and waited for Serenity to sit down. "You've always had beautiful hair. But this style suits you."

Serenity sipped at the glass of unsweetened iced tea she'd been handed as she enjoyed the sounds of her Mom and Grams around her. She hadn't realized how quiet their little house in the city was until now.

"So Grams, what have you been doing over at the Senior Center since I've been gone?"

In the spring, she and Mom saw an ad in the paper for an event at the Kitner Senior Center. As soon as they read about the couponing club, they knew Grams would love it.

Convincing her to go was a different matter entirely. Grams objected, saying the last thing she needed to do was hang out with a bunch of old fogies. Serenity still had to hide a smile at the memory.

Once she'd attended the coupon group, Grams regularly went to other events as well.

"I've invited a friend over for dinner tonight." The announcement from Grams resulted in a unanimous pause around the room.

Serenity raised an eyebrow at Mom who was sitting across from her.

Mom offered a little shrug. "That's fine, Mom. Is

this a friend you've met at the Senior Center?"

"Yes." A bright blush colored Grams' cheeks. "His name is Peter."

Serenity didn't think she'd ever seen Grams get embarrassed like this before. At a complete loss for words, she waited for Mom to say something.

And it didn't take long. Mom set her tea down on the coffee table. "I…We…Is Peter a friend?"

Grams hesitated. "We've started courting."

"Courting?!" Mom coughed and used a fist to hit her chest. "When did this happen?"

"Now, Patty. What matters is that it's serious enough to meet each other's families. The least you can do is welcome him."

Mom looked surprised. "Of course he's welcome to come here. Anytime."

Serenity couldn't blame her for being shocked. She felt it, too. "I can't wait to meet him, Grams."

"Thank you." Grams gave her a smile and turned her attention to Mom.

"Me, too. It's been a long time since Dad… You deserve to find someone. To be happy."

Grams gave her a watery smile. "Thank you, sweetie." She fingered the locket around her neck. "My Nicholas will never be forgotten. But I'm learning I might have some room left in my heart for Peter."

The tears in Grams' eyes were like a trigger, and Serenity blinked her own moisture away. She'd been a kid when Gramps had passed. The entire family had mourned the loss for many years and still remembered him with fun stories and recollections.

It was hard to imagine Grams falling in love with someone else. But if anyone deserved to be happy and have a second chance at love, it was her.

Serenity had managed to push Aaron from her thoughts for a whole ten minutes before the image of his handsome face came crashing back in. It was too bad she couldn't imagine ever finding that true love for herself. What did it say about her that Grams was likely going to find someone to spend the rest of her life with before Serenity even got close?

No, she wasn't going to go there. Not right now, anyway. She'd have plenty of time for a pity party on the drive back home tomorrow. For now, she planned on enjoying the time she got to spend with her family.

Several hours later, the rest of the family began to arrive at the Chandler home. Serenity received multiple compliments on her hair. She was sitting on the couch with Laurie, whose baby bump was starting to show.

Laurie put her hand on it and smiled. "I'm finally starting to feel a little better. I have my moments when I want to curl up and sleep the day away. But at least I'm not getting sick constantly."

Lance plopped down on the other side of Serenity. "My sister, Marian, was sick all the time like that, too. She was miserable. When Avalon was pregnant, she worried she was going to feel as bad."

Serenity had only met Lance's younger sibling a handful of times, but she always enjoyed talking to her. "How're Avalon, Duke, and baby Lorelei Grace?"

Lance grinned. "They're good. Settled into Kitner. Duke likes his job and Lorelei is absolutely adorable." He took his phone out and pulled up a photo to show them. The chubby baby with wisps of black hair and dark eyes smiled.

Laurie's face became wistful. "I wonder what this little one's going to look like."

Tuck stepped to the side of the couch beside her,

taking one of her hands in his. "I hope he or she has red, wavy hair like my beautiful wife."

The doorbell rang then, and nearly everyone in the room turned towards it.

Grams shooed them all away. "Would you all pretend to be civilized people instead of vultures waiting for the kill?"

They obeyed, but laughter followed Grams to the door. Serenity craned her neck to see her admit their guest into the house. Peter offered Grams his arm and she took it, something Serenity found especially sweet.

Grams motioned around the room. "Everyone, this is Peter Quintin."

Peter nodded at each person as she introduced them. His hair was white and closely cropped. His blue eyes were friendly and open. He stood straight and offered them a smile. "It's good to meet you all. Rose has told me a lot about you. I appreciate your welcoming an old stranger in to celebrate this beautiful woman's birthday. I hear these family meals are a bit famous around here."

Serenity enjoyed watching Grams as she patted his arm.

Laurie elbowed Serenity. "I have to admit, they're a cute couple," she said, barely above a whisper.

"I know!" Serenity smiled. "Grams seems happy."

"She really does."

Both women observed as Grams retrieved some cold water for Peter and set it just right on the coffee table. They didn't miss how he gave her a wink and reached for her hand when she moved to sit next to him.

Serenity sighed. When she spotted Lexi throwing a concerned look her way, she straightened her spine and made sure the smile she was wearing earlier was back in place.

Apparently it wasn't quick enough. A few moments later, Lexi cupped her elbow and pulled her to stand, directing her outside to the back porch.

They barely made it through the door before Lexi began. "Spill it, Serenity. You've been telling everyone you're fine since you got here, but we know you way too well." She stood with her hands on her hips. "Mom's starting to worry."

Serenity bit back a groan. She hadn't told any of her family members about her short-lived relationship with Aaron and at this point hoped to avoid it completely. Obviously her original plans weren't going to hold up.

She motioned for Lexi to take a seat and then claimed one of the deck chairs for herself.

Lexi pinned Serenity with her best big sister stare. "What's going on?"

Serenity took a deep breath to organize her thoughts and began to relate how she met Aaron and everything that had happened since then.

Aside from the occasional "Wow" or "Oh, no!" Lexi stayed silent until Serenity finished her story.

"I had no idea you moved and took up a role in a soap opera."

Serenity let the back of her head bounce off the chair backing behind her. "Seriously? And you wonder why I didn't say anything to you guys. I should have refused to spill my guts to you."

"We love you. You know that, right?"

"Yeah, I do." Serenity closed her eyes. "I'm starting to wonder if I should've stayed in Kitner."

"Serenity?"

"What?"

"Suck it up, Buttercup."

Serenity chuckled. "You channeling Grams now?"

Lexi laughed. "Maybe. Is it working?"

It was no secret among her family members that Serenity tended to internalize everything until she was ready to explode. "A little." She paused. "A man was finally interested in me for who I am and it falls apart." The story of her life, it seemed. "Remind me of this moment the next time I'm coaxed into opening up my heart. It's not worth it."

"One of these times it will be."

Serenity wanted to believe that.

Lexi stared at her hard, making Serenity uncomfortable. "What?"

"Are you in love with him?"

Serenity blinked at her as she tried to digest her sister's words. "Impossible." She crossed her arms.

Lexi raised an eyebrow. "Why?"

Was she serious? "Maybe because I've known him for all of six weeks. Or maybe because, with everything else stacked against us, it's obviously not meant to be."

"If your job wasn't on the line, would you go for it?" Serenity must not have answered fast enough because Lexi kicked the bottom of her shoe. "Well, would you?"

Out of nowhere, tears sprang to Serenity's eyes. If she didn't have to worry about her job, you bet she would. She nodded. "I'd look around for another job, except that's not the problem. It's because I'm Gideon's mom. I'd have to find another school for him, and I'm not going to do that. I can already tell Hope is the right place for him. And I'd never ask Aaron to leave. Working at Hope is his career and he loves the kids. They depend on him. Where does that leave us?"

Lexi leaned forward. "You're the glass is half-empty kind of person. You weren't like that before Jay."

Serenity sat up straight, her eyes narrowing. "Don't start with that."

"You're such a compassionate, intelligent woman. You're an amazing mom. I don't understand why you can't see that in yourself. You spend your life waiting for the other shoe to drop." Lexi reached over and put a hand on Serenity's arm. "If there's one thing I've always wished for you, it's that you'd have a little faith in yourself. It's still my hope."

Tears fell then and Serenity pushed down her frustration. She was sick and tired of crying. Part of her wanted to tell Lexi to mind her own business. But a piece of the armor around her heart broke away — a shield she hadn't even realized was in place.

"I'm not sure I know how to be any other way." She sniffed and used her sleeve to wipe away the wetness on her cheeks.

Lexi put an arm around Serenity's shoulder and hugged her. "It's never too late to change. I'll be praying for you." She got up and went back inside.

Alone, Serenity took the time to compose herself. The last thing she wanted to do was to go back inside and make Grams worry about her.

Lexi's words kept replaying themselves in her mind. What if she was right? When had she become a glass-half-empty kind of person? She didn't want to be like that. She wanted to be the type that could find a silver lining in everything.

"God, the way I think is as much of a habit as anything else. Please remind me as I go through my day to look at the bright side of things."

Her mind went to Aaron and their situation. Where was the silver lining in that? Grams' voice came to mind. *Absence makes the heart grow fonder.*

Seriously? How cliché was that?

Except, when she realized she was reacting simply to the thought of him, she wondered if it might be true. Was he feeling the same way?

Chapter Eighteen

Serenity went into work Monday and wavered between longing to see Aaron again and dreading the thought of having to feign disinterest in front of everyone else.

From the moment he walked into the breakroom at lunch, the air nearly sparked with the energy they shared. How was she supposed to go back to being just friends when she wanted to feel his hand around hers?

Once they were seated and eating, he gave her a smile. "I see you left a part of you behind."

It took her a minute before she reached up and touched her hair with a chuckle. "Yes, I felt like it was about time. It's definitely taking some getting used to."

His eyes held hers. "It's beautiful."

"Thank you." Serenity's face warmed.

"Did you have a good time in Kitner?"

She welcomed the change in topic. "I did. It was nice going back. Grams had a great birthday party and I got to meet her new suitor."

"Really? A suitor? Good for Grams."

Serenity chuckled. "It's been a long time since

Gramps passed away. I'm glad she has a second chance at happiness like this."

"How'd Gideon do with everything? Did it shake him up at all having to come back again?" Aaron jabbed a fork into his re-heated pasta.

"I was a little worried about that. But he did fine and looked forward to getting back to his room again. He had a great time seeing everyone, though. Especially Tuck." She withdrew a chip from the bag on the table and tossed it into her mouth. "They've always been close and Gideon's really missed him."

"They're lucky to have each other."

She gave a nod in what she hoped expressed her appreciation for his comment. Despite how things turned out between her and Aaron, it'd been worth moving there for the chance to meet him. Because even if nothing ever went further than it did right now, she would never forget how he'd made her feel.

Tears burned in her throat. She tried to blink them — and her thoughts — away but wasn't fast enough. Aaron must have seen something in her eyes because now he was watching her, concern etched into his features.

"Serenity?"

She raised a hand to stop him. "Please, don't. I'm fine." Her eyes darted to the door as someone stepped in. She hadn't realized how nervous she was to have Cynthia see them together until the sense of relief she felt when it wasn't her.

She hated this. Every minute of it. Because the one thing she wanted more than anything at that moment was the freedom to accept Aaron's comforting embrace. She craved the strength and safety that it was sure to surround her with.

Aaron didn't seem remotely convinced but he maintained his seat and didn't try to ask her anything else. His eyes never strayed far from her face, though. He cleared his throat. "Did I hear you and Gideon are coming to the basketball game tomorrow night?"

"We're planning on it if all goes well in the afternoon. I'm not sure how late we'll stay, though."

He smiled at her. "It's not usually too late. You're sure to get a laugh or two at my expense."

"I doubt it. Letty assures me you're quite good."

"I still intend on getting you onto that court at some point." He winked at her.

"Yeah, don't hold your breath on that one."

They compared stories of playing basketball in the past until their lunch hour was up. Conversation flowed easily and it was almost as if they'd gone back to normal again. Almost.

As they were about to part ways, Aaron's expression was so intense it made her hands shake and her heart jump. He reached over, gave her arm a brief squeeze, and leaned close to her ear. "Don't give up on us yet, Serenity."

His words settled on her heart. What exactly did they mean? She pondered every possible way she could interpret them until she was ready to go insane.

~

Tuesday morning was unusually busy. Serenity was sorting through some paperwork on the desk when a shadow moved to block some of what she was reading. She looked up, completely shocked at the person grinning down at her.

"Tuck? What are you doing here?"

She stood and rushed around the desk to give him a hug. He lifted her briefly in his arms before setting her back down again. "I had a case that brought me to the area. I thought I'd come by and take my favorite little sister to lunch."

"Are you kidding? That sounds perfect! I go to lunch at one — another hour and a half. You're welcome to stick around or come back. Whatever works better for you."

Maggie spoke from her chair at the other end of the desk. "Is this the infamous brother you've been telling me about?"

Serenity blinked. "Of course! I'm sorry. Tuck, this is my co-worker and friend, Maggie. Maggie, this is my big brother, Tuck."

The two shook hands. Serenity gave Tuck a great deal of credit for not reacting to the woman's bright green fingernails or the matching eyeshadow and hair highlights. Then again, she knew he saw a whole lot more in his line of work.

"It's good to meet you, Maggie."

"You as well." Maggie turned her attention to Serenity. "We can trade lunch hours for today if you want to."

Tuck held up a hand. "The extra time will be good. I have a couple of things I want to do quickly before one. But I do appreciate your kind offer." He turned back to Serenity. "Does that work for you?"

"Yes. I have a few things I need to finish up here. And I need to let someone know I won't be there for lunch today."

"Aaron?"

Serenity's eyes widened for a moment before narrowing. "Lexi spoke with you." He shrugged.

146

"Fantastic. And yes." She shot him a glare she hoped made it clear she didn't want to talk about it right now.

"Then I'll excuse myself and I'll be back to pick you up right at one."

She gave him another hug and watched as he left the room. Before she got caught up in her paperwork again, she sent Aaron a quick text. She didn't know if he'd bring Mexican food in today like he had in the past, but she sure didn't want him to do that when she wasn't going to be there.

"He seems nice." Maggie was grinning. "I saw the wedding ring. Too bad. Do you have any other brothers?"

Serenity chuckled. "Nope, just the one. Which is probably a good thing, because I doubt I could have handled two."

~

Aaron had rounded the corner just in time to see some tall man engulf Serenity in a hug. From the joy on her face and the sparkle in her eyes, she clearly didn't object. The whole scene filled him with unease as jealousy twisted in his gut.

The last thing he wanted to do was watch the two of them interact so he headed back to his office. Who was the guy and what was he doing here? He didn't think he'd seen anyone come visit her at work before. She hadn't been in town long, where did she meet him? He didn't recognize the guy from church.

Less than ten minutes later, Aaron's phone chimed with a text. He was pretty certain who it was from.

"I'm not going to be able to meet you for lunch today. I'm sorry. Looking forward to tomorrow."

Aaron didn't think it was too much of a stretch to assume she was going out with the guy she'd been hugging only minutes ago. Despite the instinct to go and deck the guy, he remained rooted in place.

That he'd ever assumed he might be the only man she was interested in was absurd. A woman like Serenity — gorgeous, intelligent, and kind — had to have men expressing interest in her everywhere she went. What were the odds she'd choose him, especially with the added complication of their work situation?

He fought against the wave of defeat that threatened to crash over him.

~

"Did you really have a case in the area?" Serenity asked Tuck. They'd just been seated at a little diner down the street and were checking their menus.

"I did. Though it wasn't overly urgent, which gave me some of this extra time I'm taking advantage of." He motioned to her menu. "Order whatever you want. It's on me."

She smiled, appreciating his thoughtfulness. She didn't have to peruse the food choices for long. The moment she saw the BLT and fries, she'd made her decision. "And I appreciate it. It's always good to see you. I miss hanging out with you."

"I miss it, too." He gave his order to the waitress and handed her his menu. Serenity followed suit.

When the waitress disappeared, Serenity took her napkin and wadded it up before dropping it in her lap.

"How's Laurie today?"

Their waitress came back with their drinks and Tuck thanked her.

"She was doing great when I left. In fact, her energy level was making me tired." He laughed. "I'm glad she's not having as much morning sickness. That was hard to see."

Serenity nodded and took a sip of her strawberry lemonade. "I imagine so. I can't wait until you guys find out if it's a boy or a girl."

They chatted about baby stuff until their lunches were brought to them and then both quieted as they ate a few bites.

Serenity's sandwich tasted amazing. She couldn't remember the last time she'd eaten bacon. Which probably was a crime in some country or another. She nodded at Tuck. "Lexi asked you to check in on me, didn't she?"

Tuck frowned at her. "No. I decided to do that on my own."

She rolled her eyes. "I'm fine. What all did she tell you?" The moment his expression turned incredulous, she chuckled. "Never mind." There were few secrets in the Chandler family. Most of the time it was a good thing. "I'm not a love-crazed teenager. And this is nothing like Jay. I chose to put some distance between Aaron and me. I'll be fine."

"I know you will. But accepting help never hurts."

He was right. She swallowed past the catch in her throat. "Thanks," she managed to say.

"You're welcome." He pointed at her plate. "Eat."

She held up hands to stop him in mock seriousness. "Okay, okay." Her mind went to Aaron, who was likely eating lunch in the breakroom right now. It reminded her of the game later in the evening. "Hey, how long are you going to be in town? I hope your case will be easy to wrap up." She knew that he often couldn't talk about an active case and wasn't expecting any details.

Tuck shook his head. "It should've been pretty painless. I have a couple of leads I needed to check up on, but they're more like paper trails. I was hoping to get things tied up before now, but everything's taking longer than I had planned. I may need to stay tonight if I have to go back and speak to someone involved in the case tomorrow."

"You know you're welcome to stay at our house."

He ate a forkful of corn. "I appreciate that. I'll have a better idea later this afternoon. I'll call and let you know for sure."

"I promised a friend at church that Gideon and I would go to a basketball game at the gym there this evening. You're free to join us if you do end up staying."

Tuck smiled. "Sounds like fun."

Serenity was supposed to be trying to keep her distance from Aaron. Yet, here she was, counting down the hours until she got to see him tonight. He'd said he intended to get her out on the court. Thinking about it released a whole swarm of butterflies in her stomach. Though at the moment, she wasn't sure if it was in response to playing basketball for the first time in years, or the possibility of being close to Aaron while she was trying to convince herself they could be just friends.

Which, by the way, hadn't worked so far.

Chapter Nineteen

Aaron easily caught the ball Zane threw to him and rotated, passing it to another teammate who, in turn, made a two-point basket. He made an effort to not look towards the opposite end of the gym where most of the family and friends were gathered.

Zane elbowed him in the ribs. "She's still there."

"I have no idea what you're talking about."

With a guffaw, Zane shook his head. "Right. You keep telling yourself that. I'm sure you don't care one bit that she's been watching almost the entire game — and one player on our team especially. Do you want me to go ask Letty to find out who the other guy is?"

Aaron glared at the tall man who was sitting on the gym floor interacting with Gideon. A big part of him wanted to tell Zane yes. Or even better, walk over there and demand an explanation himself. "No, I don't." Because he refused to appear as jealous as he was feeling right now. Aaron dragged his focus back to the game and moved to accept an inbound ball.

The next time he was able to steal a glimpse of the

spectators, he spotted Gideon crying. Serenity was on her knees trying to comfort him, but the boy shook his head and collapsed in a heap on the floor. Aaron tried to make a shot but missed. As he jogged to the other end of the court, he could tell that Gideon was in a full meltdown and she looked frazzled. The tall man that had come to the game with Serenity bent down to pick the boy up and the three walked out of the gym together.

Aaron hoped Gideon was okay. He'd only witnessed one of the boy's meltdowns in the past and it was pretty rough. Serenity assured him that Gideon had few and he was glad of that. He was also glad she had some assistance right now, though he sure wished it was him who was doing the helping.

The game went well. Normally, he would have thoroughly enjoyed it. But tonight, his mind was centered on Serenity and Gideon, making it nearly impossible to concentrate on anything else. He grabbed his bottle of water and jogged over to where Letty was sitting. Zane was right behind him.

Zane made a show of grabbing Letty and giving her a big kiss. She squealed and tried to squirm out of his arms. "You are way too sweaty and smelly to be doing that." But the grin on her face told them all that she didn't mind a bit.

"Oh, you know you'd be lost if I didn't give you an end-of-game smooch."

Letty relaxed her body and Zane eased her backwards over his arm before giving her another kiss.

Aaron chuckled. "Okay, guys, get a room."

Zane gave him a knowing look. "You're jealous." He winked.

"Right." Maybe. Okay, yeah. He was jealous. If he

was completely honest with himself, he wished he could kiss Serenity the same way that Zane kissed Letty. But instead of hoping he could talk her into playing basketball with him, she was nowhere to be seen. He focused on Letty. "Is Gideon okay?"

She nodded. "Something bothered him and I'm not even sure Serenity could figure out what. But they had to take him outside for a while. I don't think they've left yet."

Relief tangled with concern. "I'll go see if they're okay." He was about to head out the door when he met them coming back in. He took in Serenity, the man she was with, and Gideon. The boy's eyes were red rimmed, but he was smiling and he went right to a colorful volleyball in the corner, twirling it in a circle on the floor. "I noticed you had to leave. I was hoping everything was all right."

Serenity looked tired. "It is now. I still don't completely understand what set him off. We took him out to the park and that seemed to work as a reset." She released a heavy sigh. "It's times like this when I wish he could talk and tell me what's wrong."

"I'm sorry. I'm glad he's fine now."

"So am I." Her eyes widened and she blinked at him. "Wow, I'm totally spaced out tonight. I haven't even introduced the two of you. Aaron, this is my brother, Tuck Chandler. Tuck, this is Aaron."

Serenity's brother. Of course. The similarity between the two of them was hard to miss. The dark hair, the brown eyes. Even some of the mannerisms. Now he felt like an idiot for being jealous of the guy.

Tuck put his hand out. "It's good to meet you."

"You, too." Aaron shook his hand.

Serenity jerked her chin towards the center of the

court. "I take it the game's over? I'm sorry I missed the rest. You played great, though."

"Thanks. It's a lot of fun." He took a swig from his water bottle and looked to Tuck. "I hear your sister used to play basketball. I'm hoping to convince her to go out there and play a game with us one of these weeks."

Tuck raised an eyebrow. "She used to be quite good. My hat's off to you if you can get her back on the court."

Serenity jabbed her brother in the stomach with her elbow and tossed him a disapproving glance. Her gaze flitted to her son. Gideon was sitting by the ball, his hands over his ears, and his eyes squinting. "I'd better get him home before we have a repeat performance."

Tuck nodded. "I think that's a good idea. Go ahead and take him out. I'll be there in a few minutes."

She opened her mouth and closed it again as if second guessing what she was about to say. "I'll see you at work tomorrow, Aaron. Please tell Letty and Zane goodbye for me."

"I will. You guys be careful."

She smiled, took Gideon by the hand, and left the gym. Aaron didn't take his eyes off them until they disappeared. It was then he turned his full attention on the tall man studying him.

Tuck cleared his throat. "Do you have a few moments? I have something I want to talk to you about."

"Of course." What could Tuck possibly want to talk to him about? Aaron led the way to the door and they stepped into the hall. He waited for the other man to speak first. It didn't take long.

"I'm going to cut to the chase here. You've

managed to make my sister miserable."

Wait. What? "I'm sorry?" Aaron swallowed hard. He remembered Serenity telling him her brother was a cop. Yeah, he'd guess he was good at his job, too.

"Serenity's been an emotional mess the last week and we didn't know why until this weekend. I thought that, since I was in town, I'd come meet the man that seems to be at the epicenter of her difficulties."

Was this guy serious? How did he manage to keep from blinking for so long? "She's not the only one who's been miserable. Did she tell you about the guidelines?"

"I've heard about them. But I'd like for you to explain them to me in detail."

Aaron did just that. He told Tuck about the couple that caused the issues in the first place, about how Cynthia had let everyone know about the new policy, and then how she'd summoned Serenity to her office.

Tuck seemed thoughtful. "And you say the board voted this through? It seems a bit of a stretch."

"I agree. But here we are." Aaron wished he knew what the man was thinking. He was allowing little emotion to show on his face.

Tuck shifted his weight, his gaze intense. "And what are you going to do about it?"

"There's a quarterly board meeting scheduled in a couple of weeks. It's open to the public and I'm going to attend. I want to speak with them and see if we can't remove the guidelines from the school's policy."

"Have you told Serenity about this?"

Aaron had wanted to talk with the board first. He figured if it solved their problems, great. If not, he was going to have to decide what to do next. "I have not."

The cop's eyes pinned him in place. "And what plan

do you have should they decide to leave the guideline as it is?"

"I plan to weigh my options then. But looking for another job is among them."

Tuck sat up straight again and gave a firm nod. "Good man. In that case, I may be able to help. Keep your plans and I'll do some digging."

Aaron got the feeling that he'd passed whatever test Tuck had put him through. He was still trying to catch up with it all. But if the man was offering his help in getting the board to change the guidelines, Aaron wasn't about to turn that down. "Any assistance you can lend would be greatly appreciated." He reached out and shook Tuck's hand for the second time. "For the record. I'd do anything in my power to make your sister happy."

~

By the time the weekend rolled around, Serenity was more than ready. She was tired of trying to find some kind of balance with Aaron at work. When they spoke, things were friendly. Yet she was constantly peeking over her shoulder, half expecting Cynthia to be there.

It was so bad that twice she felt like someone was watching her and Gideon in the parking lot. While she was certain it was her own imagination, it'd been nerve wracking.

Serenity heard the mailman and retrieved the mail from the box near the front door. She leafed through the junk until the hospital's name on an envelope made her gut drop to her shoes. Dreading what she'd find, she opened it and unfolded the paper.

The fees they were charging for Gideon's ER visit

was even more than what she'd expected it to be. But the amount she owed jumped off the page like a neon sign: $0.00. The bill had been paid in full. But by whom? Her eyes scanned the page but found no information to satisfy her desperate curiosity.

She withdrew her phone and called the hospital. After talking to several different people, she finally discovered that someone had come in several days after Gideon had received treatment and paid the balance using cash. He or she had done so anonymously and no one could even give her a hint of who it could have been.

Frustrated at the lack of answers, she ran through the list of people who might have gone back to pay the bill. Aaron came to mind first. That he might have taken care of it resulted in a jumble of emotions. Part of her was flattered that he would do something so thoughtful. But it was a lot of money and a bigger part of her didn't appreciate that he might have done this without talking to her first. It kicked her need to be in control of her life into high gear.

She was about to dial his number when her mind drifted to her family. Taking care of the bill was something Tuck or Lexi would do, too. Even Lance would be tempted. But walking in and paying cash? She doubted it. She supposed it might have been Letty or Maggie. But no matter how many other people she considered, Aaron's name kept moving to the top of the list.

She punched in his number and waited through the rings until he picked up.

"Hey, Serenity. Is everything okay?"

"I was hoping you could tell me that." His lack of response made her assume he was surprised by her brusque tone of voice and she felt bad. If he was the one who paid the bill, it was still a genuinely kind thing to do, even though she'd rather he hadn't. "I'm sorry. I got the statement from the hospital after Gideon was hurt. Someone walked in and paid the entire balance in full. With cash." She paused, hoping he'd jump in. When he didn't, she sighed. "Was it you, Aaron?"

"I'm not going to lie. I thought about it. But I knew you'd be upset if I did. Am I wrong?"

"No, you're not wrong." She swallowed, mentally crossing him off the list. "You're the first person I thought of who might have paid the bill. I don't know whether to apologize for that or not."

"Don't." He was silent for a time. "You know that if you ever needed anything, I'd help you in a heartbeat. Right?"

"Yeah, I know." Her voice sounded breathless to her own ears. "Thanks for being honest with me. I should probably go."

"Okay. I hope I'll see you tomorrow at church."

"Bye, Aaron."

"Bye, Serenity."

She hung up but continued to stare at the photo of him she'd added to his contact information. A moment later, she dialed Tuck's number.

"Hi, little sister. To what do I owe the pleasure of your call?" Humor laced his deep voice.

"Wow, you're in a good mood."

"I ought to be. I get to hang out with my beautiful wife all day. And she's in a baking mood. Do you know what that means?" He sounded so hopeful, Serenity had to chuckle.

"You're getting a whole bunch of sweets."

"You bet I am." He spoke to Laurie in the

background before returning to the phone. "Seriously, though, what's up?"

"I've got a little problem and I thought I'd see if you could do me a favor." She told him about the hospital bill and how she'd weeded Aaron from the possible people who paid the balance. "They said someone came in a few days later. I doubt it's anyone there. But could you ask for me at family dinner tomorrow? I'd really appreciate it. I want to thank whoever did it, even though I think the person should have spoken with me first."

"Sure, I'll ask. It wasn't us, though. Not that I wouldn't have been tempted. But I knew I'd never hear the end of it from you if I did."

Serenity nodded. "You're right about that."

"Anyone else there at the school who might have done it?"

"I spoke with Aaron and he said no. I seriously doubt that any of the other people we know would have."

"I'll ask the family and call you back Monday or Tuesday."

"Thanks, Tuck. I appreciate it."

They said their goodbyes.

Gideon startled her when he ran into the room with something he needed help with. "Sure, big guy, let me see it."

He'd just gone back down the hall to his room when there was a faint knock at the door. She checked the peephole to find Letty standing there. She picked up Kia and pulled the door open before ushering her guest inside.

"Is everything okay? What are you doing here?"

Letty gave her a hug and a reserved smile. "I've been

worried about you. I don't get to visit with you much anymore and I wanted to make sure you're okay."

"I'm fine." Okay, she was stretching the truth a bit. But she didn't want to talk about the bill. Or Aaron. What else was she going to do?

"Are you going to come to church on Sunday?"

"Probably." Serenity's voice sounded much more certain than she felt. She'd planned on going, but was dreading the unavoidable awkwardness that would come with it when Aaron sat down after worship.

"Well, that sounded convincing. Are you doing all right?" Letty reached for Kia and smiled when the kitten rubbed against her chin.

"I'm fine." She leaned against the wall and crossed her arms in front of her. "Everyone keeps asking me that lately."

"Aaron keeps telling Zane he's fine, too. I personally don't believe either of you." Letty gave her a stern look. "This whole thing with the guidelines is a bump in the road. I hope you know that."

Serenity wanted to say that she doubted it. But she'd been trying hard to not be as negative. Instead, she swallowed her initial response. "I truly want to believe that. But we're stuck between a rock and a hard place. I can't take Gideon out of school and Aaron would refuse to let me if I tried. And there's no way I'd ask him to give up his job. There's not an easy answer. We're doing our best to keep on keeping on."

"I don't know if I'm supposed to tell you this or not. But Aaron's going to the board in a couple of weeks. He obviously hasn't given up. And a guy willing to stand up to Cynthia ... Well, let's just say he gets a lot of respect from me."

Serenity thought about what Letty had said. She was

right. If Aaron was planning on going to the board and challenging Cynthia's policy, he clearly thought their relationship was worth fighting for. She still couldn't shake the worry that, once the board officially knew about them, they might have her fired as well. If only she knew whether or not that was a possibility...

She didn't want her friend to worry further and forced a smile. "Thanks, Letty."

"You're welcome." She put the kitten on the floor and gave Serenity another hug. "See you tomorrow?"

"Tomorrow."

Chapter Twenty

On Sunday morning, Gideon was excited to go back to church again. Serenity was glad he liked his class so well and wished she could share his enthusiasm. Her stomach was tied up in knots and Serenity hoped she could make it through the service. She realized she might have to start sitting apart from her friends so she could focus more on the service and less on the issues between her and Aaron. The entire drive there, she alternated between trying to psych herself up and talk herself into turning around and going home again.

She got Gideon settled in his class before joining Letty and Zane. Both gave her a sympathetic look which she didn't need when she was hanging onto her sanity by a fingernail.

Worship began and she did her best to focus on the songs and singing her praises. Aaron was in the back where he usually played the keyboard and that made it easier to ignore his presence.

Until he stepped forward and cleared his throat. "This week has been a challenge for me. I don't know about the rest of you, but when that happens, I often struggle for control. Control over the circumstance, control over the emotions I'm fighting, and even control over how I want God to respond to my problems."

At that last part, a number of people in the congregation chuckled. Serenity didn't join in, but his words struck her with an invisible force that made her suck in a breath of air. What he described was exactly what she'd been going through this week. Aaron's deep voice pulled her focus back to him.

"I heard this song in the car the other day and I felt like God had put it on the radio for me. This is a song by Casting Crowns and it's called 'Just Be Held'. I want to share it with you all this morning."

Someone handed Aaron a guitar and his long fingers began to play a tune as the rest of the worship team joined in.

The words of the song flowed into Serenity's heart, taking residence in the confused and lonely corridors within. She didn't realize she was crying until a tear fell from her chin and landed on her arm. The box of tissues under the chair in front of her beckoned but she didn't want Letty to see how emotional she was. Serenity did her best to swipe away the tears with her hands and sniffed. When she looked up again, she found Aaron's eyes on her as he ended the song.

Worship continued for another ten minutes, giving her a chance to get her tears under control before Aaron joined them. Instead of going past her and Letty, he stopped and claimed the seat next to Serenity.

His arm brushed hers and Serenity fought the need to lean into him. She succeeded until he bowed his head low enough to whisper in her ear, his scent enveloping her. "I miss you."

Tears sprang to her eyes again. "I miss you, too."

He reached for her hand and held it gently in his, lacing their fingers together. The pad of his thumb stroked hers. He released a lungful of air he must have been holding. Serenity surrendered and leaned against his arm, drawing from him the strength she'd needed so badly.

~

Aaron had spent a lot of time in the last two weeks praying. He'd struggled with himself, desperately seeking an answer to their problem. Every time he thought he might have a solution, something would step in the way.

That song the other day had gone a long way towards bringing him peace. Even though it would be nice if God would hand out maps to go along with His plans, he finally realized he didn't have to figure it out all on his own.

But it wasn't until he saw Serenity's face in the congregation while he sang that Aaron knew everything was going to work itself out. It had to.

When Serenity rested her cheek against his arm, he realized he was falling in love with her. Or maybe he already had.

There was no way he could concentrate on the message. He desperately needed to talk with Serenity and it'd be hard to do once Gideon was out of his Bible school class.

Aaron leaned down again, her hair brushing against his face. "Can we go and talk? Please?"

Serenity turned to Letty and said something,

although it was too quiet for Aaron to make out the words. A moment later, she gave him a nod and moved to stand. He continued to hold her hand as he led them out of the room and into the hall outside.

"I told Letty we'd be out front. She said she and Zane will get Gideon when church is over and bring him to us." Serenity's chocolate eyes were a whirlpool of emotion.

Taking his cue from her, Aaron led them to the front of the building. The church had stood in that same place for years with a number of tall trees around it. In one location, a stone bench waited in the shade of an especially full mimosa tree. Both of them sat down when they reached it and Aaron reluctantly released her hand.

Two weeks of wishing he could talk to her like they used to. Fourteen long days, wondering if he'd get to hold her again. And now he couldn't figure out what to say. "The last couple of weeks have felt like a lifetime."

"Yes, they have." She kept her gaze on the landscape before them.

It gave Aaron the perfect opportunity to study her profile. He loved that she wore little to no makeup and was gorgeous. Her long eyelashes curled a bit at the tips. He had a feeling they were the envy of many of her classmates in school. Serenity sat with her palms on the bench seat, fingers gripping the edge. It was the only evidence suggesting she felt as uncertain as he did.

"How've you been since you got back from Kitner. Did it make you more homesick?" One of the many things he'd worried about when she was gone was that she'd decide to move back. Now he held his breath, waiting for her response.

"You know, I kind of thought it would. And it was nice to see everyone. But Gideon and I, our lives are here now. It's not easy sometimes, but it's where we need to be." Serenity looked down at her shoes as she swung them back and forth, then turned her head towards him. "There's a lot to come back to here."

Aaron's heart thundered in his chest, each beat echoing in his ears. "I'm glad. I missed you both." That didn't even cover how he'd felt. It'd been torture, pure and simple. Even sitting beside her now and not touching her was difficult. But he didn't want to rush her. He had to know they were on the same page first.

Serenity released her hold on the bench and leaned against the back. She clasped her hands in her lap and then started to pick at one of her thumbnails. "I hate this, Aaron."

He turned, bending his knee closest to her and resting it on the seat. He let his arm lay along the top of the bench. The breeze blew strands of her hair, making them dance along his arm.

"I do, too." He said a silent prayer for the right words to say and the strength to hear her response. "I'll always be your friend. I hope you know that. If you ever need anything, all you have to do is ask. But you're more than a friend to me. Regardless of what we do to try and step back in time, that's not going to change."

Serenity's eyes slid closed, her dark lashes in contrast to her skin. She took a deep breath. When she opened them again, she fixed him with a determined look. "I can't ask you to risk your job, Aaron. That would be selfish."

"You're not. I've thought about it a lot — probably way too much — and I think Cynthia's bluffing. I don't think she'd let me go. I've been at Hope for years and the kids all know me. She wants to be in control and this is her way of trying to exercise that." He allowed his thumb to rub the top of her shoulder. Losing his job was a possibility, but he hadn't allowed himself to go there. Not yet.

She shook her head and stood before walking over to the trunk of the mimosa tree. After plucking a blade of grass, she leaned with one shoulder against the bark. "But you enjoy working at Hope. You told me that. And there's absolutely no guarantee you could get another job. What if you have to move to another town in order to find one?"

Aaron rose slowly and approached her. "You're right. I can't imagine working anywhere else. I don't want that to change. I like my job and the kids I work with. But it's you I'm falling in love with."

She inhaled sharply, the blade of grass dropping from her fingers to land at her feet.

He moved to stand in front of her and reached for her hands. "We can keep it friendly at work. There's no need to provoke Cynthia if we don't have to. But outside of the Academy … Maybe it's still a risk, but as far as I'm concerned, you and Gideon are more than worth it. I'm going to talk to the board and see if we can get things straightened out. I spoke with Tuck after the basketball game. He's trying to gather information that'll help us. We can deal with what comes after that." He gently held her chin between his thumb and finger. "Compared to losing you, it's a risk I'm willing to take."

Aaron watched her face as she processed his words. He knew how he was feeling. But what about her? The moment remained in suspended animation and he wasn't sure he was going to be able to breathe until she responded.

The emotion in her eyes pulled at his heart. "I can't stand the idea of losing you over all of this, either." Her lashes fluttered.

"We're doing this?"

Serenity's voice was breathless. "Yeah, we're doing this."

"Thank God." He tugged her into his arms and held her close. With his face buried in her hair, her scent surrounded him. He'd missed this. Everything about her.

Her arms tightened around his waist as she leaned into his chest for several heartbeats. She lifted her head to look at him.

Aaron absorbed the moment before leaning down to cover her lips with his. He wasn't sure how long he'd been kissing her when voices broke through their bubble. A few people had exited the church, but they seemed to be the only ones. "Come on, they'll be out soon." He took her hand and led her back to the bench. They sat down again. But this time, their hands remained linked.

It wasn't long before Letty, Zane, and Gideon joined the sea of people coming out of the church. Serenity waved at them and Gideon took off across the grass to crash into her. She tickled him and pulled him onto the bench beside her. "How was children's church? Did you learn a bunch?"

Letty handed her two pages that he'd done in his class. She gave Serenity a knowing look. "Everything's okay?"

"Yeah." Serenity nudged Aaron's shoulder with her own. "Everything's fine."

He swore her smile was brighter than the Texas sun.

~

Two days later, Serenity had been working a few hours when she got a text from Aaron. A check of the time told her Gideon should be with him for music therapy.

"Come to the music room. Be quiet coming in. You have to see something Gideon's doing. :-)"

The office was virtually empty so she told Maggie she was going to take a break and would be back shortly.

She walked as quickly as she could down the hallway to the music room. She slowed when she came to the door to Aaron's classroom. She could hear music playing and peeked her head around the corner. Gideon's back was to her and Aaron was sitting on the floor in front of him. Aaron noticed her immediately and gave her a subtle nod.

She leaned against the doorframe and watched silently as Aaron picked up one of the hand bells that were lined up between them. As the tune continued from the CD player on the table, Aaron rang the bell and then sang out the note. "Aaaaaaaa." He continued through the line of bells, singing each note as he went. When he reached the end, he patted Gideon's chest. "It's your turn. Gideon's turn."

Serenity had no idea what to expect. But when Gideon picked up that first bell and she heard his little voice sing the A note, tears instantly filled her eyes. He'd made sounds before and one note wouldn't have been a major thing. But when he went on to do the same for B, her heart began to pound and tears streaked down her cheek. She didn't care one bit. Her son was communicating verbally. It may only be notes, but it was huge.

His voice was beautiful. Perfect.

She listened as he sang each note. After the last bell, Aaron clapped and cheered. "Fantastic job, Gideon. You've got a great singing voice." He motioned for Serenity to approach them. "Look, your mom got to listen to you sing."

Serenity swiped away the tears and replaced them with a smile. That's all she wanted her son to see when he turned around. He was thrilled with himself. She hurried forward and knelt down beside him. "Gideon, that was amazing. I'm proud of you, big guy. So very proud of you." She reached for him and hugged him. Watching Aaron over her son's head, she mouthed, "Thank you."

"You're welcome."

She was pretty sure she saw moisture in his eyes as well.

~

Serenity felt as though she were floating on cloud nine all day after listening to Gideon sing the notes. As soon as they got home, she'd called her mom and Grams to tell them about it. Now she was on the phone with Tuck. He'd been about as excited as she had to hear the news.

"I wish I could have heard him myself."

"I'm going to ask Aaron if he can record it next week and send it to me. I should have done that today, but I was too mesmerized to even consider the option. I don't think I'll forget that moment as long as I live." She'd lost track of how many times she'd come close to tears throughout the day.

"Tell Gideon I'm really proud of him."

"I will, Tuck."

"Hey, while I've got you on the phone, I wanted to let you know I talked to the rest of the family about the hospital bill. No one here paid it."

Then who had? Because it made little to no sense. The odds that a random stranger walked up and paid her bill were pretty small. "The whole thing is driving me crazy."

"I definitely get that. Maybe it was some kind person who saw you come in. You hear of that happening once in a while. Someone trying to pay it forward." Tuck didn't sound that convinced.

Serenity wasn't either. "Maybe. I know things like that happen in real life once in a while. It's a little hard to believe."

"Well, if you have any other problems, you know to call me, right?"

"Of course. Thank you again, Tuck. I appreciate it. I don't know what I'd do without you."

"You be careful. Have you seen the forecast? They're predicting nasty weather Wednesday and Thursday up in your area. Lots of severe thunderstorms."

"We'll keep an eye on the weather. You guys do the same."

They hung up. Serenity played the scene in the music room through her mind one more time and grinned. She dialed Lexi's number to tell her all about it. She might share the latest concerning her Music Man as well.

Chapter Twenty-One

Serenity cast a furtive glance at the sky as she ushered Gideon into the car Thursday morning. The weather Tuck had warned her about wasn't bad yesterday. They'd had a lot of rain and a couple of thunderstorms. Nothing to write home about. But this morning already promised more.

The sky above her was blue. But a wall of clouds was rolling in from the horizon and they were nearly black. The air was still and warm, which usually wasn't a good sign when a storm was approaching.

At least at the school, she and Maggie could keep the radio on while they worked. They'd be sure to hear updates throughout the day.

She was about to pull away from the house when the hair on the back of her neck stood on end. The sensation of being watched flowed through her. Serenity made sure the doors were locked and craned her neck to peer up and down the street. Nothing. It was an impression she'd started to get several times a week and she was beginning to wonder if she was getting neurotic.

They were going to be late if she didn't get on the road. Pushing thoughts of being watched from her head, she studied the wall clouds as she moved towards Hope Academy.

She saw Aaron in the parking lot and waved as she found a space. He walked towards them. "Good morning, you two. How are you?"

"A little rushed but well. How about you?" Serenity resisted the urge to reach for his hand or step on her tiptoes for a kiss. They'd been playing it cool at work all week. At least she hoped they had. Cynthia hadn't spoken to either of them again and Serenity chose to believe it was because they were flying under the radar.

"I'm better now." He gave her a wink. "I don't like the look of that sky." Aaron nodded towards the wall clouds that were visibly moving closer.

They hurried into the building and waved their goodbyes. Serenity held Gideon's hand as they headed for his classroom. A low rumble of thunder sounded and her gaze flew to his face. He must not have heard it because he kept walking as he took in everything around him.

He'd been afraid of thunder for several years now. During the day, it wasn't quite as bad because at least there were other things for him to focus on. But if a storm hit at night, it meant being up and keeping him comforted and distracted until the storm was over.

She'd warned Letty about it yesterday and was happy to hear that he'd never reacted to the thunder. But if the clouds outside were any indication, today might be a different story.

When they got to his classroom, she reminded Letty of Gideon's fear, gave him a hug, and headed to the front office.

Maggie already had the radio tuned to the weather station and was conversing with a parent about it. "Yes, we do have a storm room. If a tornado warning is sounded, all of the teachers know to take the kids there."

That seemed to satisfy the parent. She thanked Maggie and hurried towards the parking lot.

Serenity put her bag in a drawer and sat down as a louder clap of thunder sounded. Her thoughts immediately flew to Gideon. When it came to storms, she'd rather be with him. It was easier than worrying about whether he was scared or not. She knew Letty would text or call if she needed to go get him. Still...

Maggie's voice broke into her thoughts. "Good morning."

"Good morning." Serenity looked at her friend for the first time. Had she planned the blueish gray outfit or was it a coincidence that it matched the storm so well? Serenity indicated the radio. "Anything interesting yet?"

"They've got us under a severe thunderstorm watch and a tornado watch until eight tonight."

Watches weren't at all unusual for this area of Texas but they still made Serenity cringe. "Lovely."

"Right?"

This particular storm came through with quite a bit of thunder and then disappeared by mid-morning. Serenity texted Letty to make sure Gideon was okay. Letty assured her he was. Serenity sighed with relief. They enjoyed a couple hours of calm before the next storm made its approach around lunch. At the first sound of thunder, Serenity groaned. She was staring out the window when Aaron walked into the breakroom.

"How's it looking out there?"

She shrugged. "Nasty. I hate storms like this. Gideon gets nervous during them."

Aaron set his stuff on their table and moved to stand next to her. "I don't think he's the only one." He took in the clouds outside and withdrew his phone. As if on cue, it sounded loudly. "I have an app on here that tells me about any warnings. They just issued a severe thunderstorm warning for our area for the next forty minutes."

"What app is that?" He told her and she downloaded it to her phone, too. It would certainly be helpful, especially for any alerts at night.

They sat down to eat. Several times, thunder interrupted their conversation and once, it was loud enough to shake the building.

~

Serenity was so tense that Aaron kept wishing he had permission to hold her hand or even wrap his arms around her. The rain started to fall and before long, they could hear the pings of hail hitting the window. In unison, they moved to observe through the glass.

The hail itself wasn't large — maybe the size of a pea. But it was the sky that was ominous. Billowing clouds were black with a green tinge to them. He'd only seen a sky like that a handful of times, but it rarely meant anything good. Thunder shook the building. "Come on, let's go find Gideon so you can make sure he's all right. This is only going to get louder. If you need to stay with him until it's over, I'm sure everyone would understand."

Serenity nodded. She shoved the last of her sandwich and chips into the trash can and led the way into the hall. More thunder echoed and the lights flickered before going out completely. Serenity reached for her keys and pulled them out of her pocket. There was a small flashlight on a keyring and she turned it on. Aaron chose the flashlight application on his phone to help illuminate the way.

He kept expecting the lights to come back on and when they didn't, his need to get Serenity reunited with her son intensified.

They hadn't gotten far when they ran into Letty. The moment the teacher saw them, her face morphed from worry to relief, then back to worry again. "I was looking for you. We had the kids at the bathrooms after lunch before going back to the classroom. The lights went out and all the kids were screaming. By the time we got them out and located a flashlight, we couldn't find Gideon."

Aaron reached for Serenity's hand and held it tight. Right now, he couldn't care less that they were standing in the middle of the school.

"You can't find him? You're sure he wasn't hiding in the bathroom?" Serenity's voice had risen a notch and she clutched at his hand.

"I'm positive."

Aaron felt as though someone punched him in the gut as he flashed back to when his brother had wandered. He remembered his parents discussing the places they looked and where Kenneth might be. As a child, he'd tried to rack his brain and figure out where Kenneth might have been hiding. Watching his parents go from concerned to terrified was one of the many things he'd had nightmares about growing up.

Now he could see the range of emotions play across Serenity's face. He expected fear to well up inside him. Instead, it was anger. He was not going to lose Gideon, not like this. *God, protect that boy and lead us to him.*

He spotted Zane dodging a number of people in the hallway as he approached them. He handed a large flashlight to each of them and kept one for himself. "Letty, I'll help them find Gideon. Go ahead and get back to your class. They're in the library with the aides, right?"

Letty nodded and disappeared into the darkness.

Aaron put his phone in his back pocket and gripped the flashlight. He gave Serenity's hand a reassuring squeeze. "Do you have any idea where he'd go if he were scared?"

"He'd go somewhere familiar. His classroom, your music room. Maybe the car, though I don't think he'd go outside in this weather."

Zane shook his head. "We're not taking any chances. I'm going to check outside and give Maggie a heads-up — make sure no one goes out there alone."

Aaron clapped him on the shoulder. "Thanks, man. We'll check the other places. Be careful."

"You, too."

The school was dark except for the light filtering through the windows as Aaron and Serenity made their way down the maze of hallways to Letty's classroom. They searched everywhere but found no sign of Gideon. Where was he?

Serenity slumped forward and he was afraid she was going to break down crying. But she straightened her spine again and rolled her shoulders back. "Come on. Let's go check your classroom."

Aaron had a surge of respect for her control. They

re-entered the hallway as a whine filled the air. At the same time, both of their phones sounded an alarm. Aaron whipped his out.

"Tornado warning. We need to find Gideon and get to the safe room." He grabbed her hand again and pulled her into the hallway that was now swarming with students and teachers alike.

As they shined their lights around the music room, shadows cast on the walls gave an eerie feel. The siren continued to sound.

"Gideon!" Serenity's voice echoed off the walls. "Gideon, it's Mommy. Come on, we're going to go somewhere safe and away from all this noise."

They waited, hoping for a sign to tell them he was there. Aaron moved to check under his desk and the table. He'd held so much hope that they'd find him there. When they saw no sign of him, urgency kicked up a notch. He hated not knowing where the tornado warning was originating from. If it was the other side of town, they were fine. But if it were close by...

Serenity's eyes were wide. He sensed she was reaching her limit of control and he couldn't blame her. "I don't know where else to look."

"Maybe we should go up front and check with Maggie? See if we can find Zane?"

"Yeah."

They were about to walk back out the door when Aaron heard a noise. Serenity must have heard it, too, because she stopped and turned.

There it was again.

"Mmmma."

"Gideon?" She flashed her light around the room desperately. "Baby, please come out if you're in here. Come out and I'll sing you the Sunshine Song."

A pile of cushions in one corner moved. The shape of a little boy stood up and ran towards them. Serenity knelt down and gathered him into her arms, her flashlight clattering to the floor.

Relief flooded Aaron's body as he watched the two embrace. He picked up her flashlight and put an arm around them. Hail pelted the window in his classroom and wind roared outside. "Come on, we've got to get to the safe room. Let me carry Gideon."

Serenity hesitated only a moment before she handed her son over to him. He gave her his light, took her hand in his, and led the way. The safe room was just off the cafeteria and packed full of people.

"You found him. Praise God." Letty was sitting on the floor against a wall, several children huddled on her lap. "I've been praying you were all right."

Serenity took Gideon and sat down next to her. Aaron joined them.

"We're okay," she said, resting her cheek against her son's head. She leaned against Aaron's side and he put an arm around her shoulder.

Even in the room, they could hear the wind continue to roar around them, drowning out the sirens. Bangs and the sound of glass shattering punctuated the din. The air became stuffy with such a large number of people crowded within.

Aaron shifted so that Serenity rested against his chest and prayed that the storm would end soon.

Chapter Twenty-Two

Serenity welcomed the way Aaron's arms felt around her shoulders and her son sitting in her lap. Despite the threat of the tornado and the fear of the situation, knowing the people she cared about most in this town were safe in the room with her made all the difference.

Her mind went back to the music room and the relief she'd felt when she'd heard Gideon's voice.

His voice. *"Mmmma."* Goosebumps peppered her arms. "Aaron. When we found Gideon. Did he talk?"

He thought a moment then his eyes widened. He looked from the boy to his mother. "I've never heard him make sounds like that. I think he was calling you. It sounded like Ma to me."

The idea took a moment to sink in and then her heart began to race. It'd taken almost six years, but she'd finally heard her son's first word. She covered her mouth with her hand while tears rolled down her cheeks. She took a shaky breath as she put her arms around her son and held him close, kissing the top of his head.

She felt a hand on her shoulder and then heard Aaron's voice near her ear. "I think we've witnessed more than one miracle today."

Serenity nodded her head. "My son talked for the first time. Against all odds. It's a dream come true." She smiled through her tears.

He tightened his arm around her shoulder and his lips brushed against her temple.

They waited in silence for several minutes. Aaron rubbed his hand up and down her arm. "Listen. I think the storm's finally dying down."

Serenity realized the sirens were no longer going off. "How do we know it's okay to go out?"

Aaron checked his phone but shook his head. "No service."

Zane spoke from nearby. "We're going to give it ten more minutes, then Aaron and I will go out and assess the situation."

Letty didn't look too happy about that, but said nothing. Instead, she reached over and took her husband's hand.

When it was time, Serenity whispered, "Please be careful."

Aaron touched his forehead to hers. "I will. We'll be right back."

It was a tense handful of minutes as she and Letty sat next to each other, waiting for their guys to return safely. When they did, they came through the double doors and propped them open.

Zane spoke loudly, projecting his voice throughout the room. "We're clear. A lot of windows have been broken by the wind. We're going to need to keep the kids away from the glass so no one gets hurt."

Cynthia spoke from the middle of the group.

"Teachers, take your students to the cafeteria. We're going to have a lot of concerned parents coming to get their children."

Aaron moved to help Serenity to her feet. "I'm pretty sure they're going to have to close the school for a day or two. The place is a mess." He took one of Gideon's hands while Serenity took the other. "Be careful of the glass, buddy."

They followed the crowd of people out of the cramped room and into the hallway. While the electricity was still out, the lighter-colored clouds outside allowed more light through the windows.

Nearly all of the students were calm as they followed their teachers. Serenity was impressed by how well the teachers had managed to keep the kids occupied and distracted as they made their way to the cafeteria. Letty was especially good with her students, singing a song that Aaron and Serenity quickly joined in with.

Like a well-oiled machine, everyone got the kids seated at the tables and snacks were provided to help keep them occupied. Gideon was happy to nibble on apple slices and drink some chocolate milk.

Aaron and Zane had disappeared again to get some information but both promised to return. Serenity and Letty stood together, watching over the kids.

"I wonder if we actually had a tornado in the area," Letty whispered. "If this many windows broke in the school, what does it look like outside?"

Serenity tried to imagine it and couldn't. She checked her phone again, knowing that if there had been a tornado, her family was likely trying to get in contact with her. Another hour and Tuck or Lance would be on the way to check on her personally. The thought made her smile.

Ten minutes later, the men returned. The four adults spoke quietly so as not to alarm the kids.

Zane was frowning. "It was a tornado and so far, no deaths have been reported. There are some injured in the area, mostly from the high winds and the damage they caused. The tornado itself touched down just outside of the school. But the wind damage was pretty wide-spread."

Aaron's gaze passed over the room full of children. "Praise God everyone's fine. If we hadn't gotten them all into the safe room, someone would've ended up hurt." His eyes landed on Gideon and an arm went around Serenity's shoulders. "This could have been much worse."

Cynthia came into the room and held a hand up high to get everyone's attention. "Parents are starting to arrive now. We're going to work in the hallway outside this room like we do in front of the school. It may take longer, but we're going to get the kids safely to their families."

She gave some directions to several people standing next to her. "There's enough damage to the school. We're going to close for the rest of the week so we have time to get the windows repaired and figure out what other damage may have occurred. An automated call will go out to all students and their families on Sunday informing them of whether or not school will resume Monday. Please be sure to inform any parent you speak with. We'll remind everyone we catch as well."

Someone's voice came from the back of the room. "Any word on how long it'll be before the electricity is restored?"

"I'm afraid not." Cynthia shook her head. "I've heard it could take a couple of days in this area. I imagine we'll get a better update later." She took enough time to cast a stony glare in Aaron and Serenity's direction.

Everything was chaotic as parents were reunited with their kids but the staff and teachers managed to keep things moving as smoothly as possible. Before long, silence filled the cafeteria and most of the teachers sagged into chairs or against walls in relief.

Gideon grasped Serenity's hand and tugged on it, motioning towards the door.

"Yeah, big guy. Let's get home and see how our house fared."

Aaron moved to follow them. "I'll come with you guys."

"You don't need to stay here?"

"I checked on my classroom earlier. For the first time, I'm thankful it has no windows."

~

Aaron escorted them out of the school and into the parking lot. The place was such a mess, it was difficult to locate their vehicles. A number of them had been blown into each other and two had even been overturned.

Thankfully, other than the dents in the body of their cars from the hail, they seemed to be okay.

Aaron followed her to the house. Trash cans and debris littered the street. The covered porch across the street had been severely damaged. The windows in the front of their duplex were intact and Serenity hoped that meant it had made it through the storm okay.

She unlocked the door and pushed it open. The power was out in this neighborhood, too, and they were greeted by warm air from inside. At the same moment, a little furry body collided with her right shin. "Poor Kia. Come here, sweetie." She scooped the kitten up and held her to her chest. Kia always seemed happy to see them, but even more so today. Serenity's phone buzzed several times and she pulled it from her back pocket. "Text messages. I still don't seem to have service, though."

"Sometimes a text message will get through when a call can't. I'll bet they're from your family."

She read through them and nodded. "Yep. Asking if we're okay." She maneuvered Kia to the crook of her arm and texted back. "I told them we're fine but that we don't have electricity."

"I would assume it may take up to a couple of days for them to get the power back on here, too." Aaron didn't like the idea of them staying in the stuffy house. It was only going to get warmer.

Her phone buzzed again. "My mom invited us to come for the weekend." She glanced at him, her expression open.

"It's not a bad idea. I think you guys should. You'll need to take Kia with you."

Serenity texted again. "Okay. I'm going to pack a few things and we're probably going to leave pretty soon. There's a break in the storms and I don't want to get caught in one on the way there."

"You're doing the right thing. You can come back Sunday morning and the power should be back on by then."

"You could come with us."

"What?" His heart leapt at her words.

"You're likely going to be out of power for a while, too. There's no reason for you to stay here and be miserable." She paused. "Come meet my family."

"Are you serious?" He knew he was smiling and he didn't care. The grin she gave him in return told him everything he needed to know.

"Yeah. I am. We have plenty of room. You may have to sleep on the couch, but you'd be welcome to stay with us." Her eyes were hopeful and he wouldn't have told her no for anything.

"I'd like that. Why don't I go to my place and get a few things and I'll be back here in half an hour or less?"

"Sounds good." She took a step towards him and lifted her chin. "Thanks, Aaron. For helping me find my baby."

He rested his hand against her cheek and brushed his lips against hers before drawing her into a hug. *Thank you, Lord, for a happy ending today. Please continue to lead us — individually and as a couple.*

Chapter Twenty-Three

It was nearing six in the evening by the time Serenity entered Kitner and pulled up in front of the Chandler house. Aaron, who'd been happy to ride with them, jerked his chin towards the collection of cars in the driveway and along the curb. "Busy place."

A wave of sympathy went through her. "It looks like everyone came here to make sure we were okay. Lucky you — you'll get to meet them all at once."

Aaron wiped his palms on his jeans. "At least I've met Tuck already. That's bound to help. Maybe he put in a good word for me."

Serenity laughed as she helped Gideon out of his booster seat. "You'll be fine." She raised herself up on her toes and kissed his cheek. "I promise I won't let them send you packing." She gave him a wink and chuckled. They'd punched some holes in a large cardboard box for Kia to travel in and she reached inside for it. The kitten mewed pathetically. Gideon ran ahead of them to the door and was already knocking on it before Serenity and Aaron had reached the top step.

The door swung open and Mom was there, welcoming Gideon with a big hug. "Oh, sweetheart, I'm glad you're okay. I heard you were a brave boy."

Gideon flashed her a grin and ran inside.

Aaron reached for the box. "Here, let me take Kia. I have a feeling you're going to need those arms free."

The women embraced. "We're fine, Mom. I promise." Serenity smiled at Aaron. "Thanks for having us on such short notice. I brought a guest. I hope you don't mind."

"Not at all." For the first time, Mom's eyes got watery. "You must be Aaron."

"Yes, ma'am. It's nice to finally have the chance to meet you."

"You just call me Patty, and it's wonderful to meet you, too." She stepped back and held the door wide open. "Come in, you two. After everything you've been through today, you must be exhausted." Once they were inside, she took the box from Aaron. "This must be Kia. Poor kitty. Serenity, I'll go put the box in your room and let her out so she can get settled."

"Thanks, Mom. We'll bring in her bowls and litter box in a minute."

Mom had barely stepped out of their view when Serenity found herself surrounded by the rest of her family. She received hugs from everyone and introduced the gang to Aaron.

He shook hands with Tuck. "It's good to see you again."

"You, too. Welcome to Kitner."

Tuck's approving nod and the way the rest of the family accepted him into the fold warmed her heart.

Grams didn't hesitate to step forward and give

Aaron a hug. She gripped his arms and gave them a small shake. "You picked a good one, Serenity."

Serenity's face grew hot and she caught a hiked eyebrow and a grin from Lexi. "Okay, everyone. Can you let the poor guy breathe before he decides to run for the hills?"

Lance chuckled. "I think it'd take more than this crazy family for that to happen."

Aaron grinned. "You're right about that."

They got everything into the house and Kia set up. Tuck and Laurie had picked up sandwiches on the way so they fixed some plates and settled into the living room. Everyone wanted to hear about the storm.

Aaron and Serenity took turns giving them the details. There wasn't a dry eye in the room when she told them about Gideon's first word.

They'd just finished talking about the broken windows when there was a loud knock at the door.

Laurie crossed her arms in front of her and rested them on her growing belly. "I thought everyone in Kitner was already here."

Laughs followed Mom as she went to answer the door. She pulled it open and gasped.

A man's voice floated into the room. "Are they here? Are they okay?"

The source of the words stepped past Mom and into the living room. Serenity rose from her spot on the couch, barely aware of her own movements. "Jay?" What was he doing here? She hadn't seen the guy in over six years. She glanced around the room, relieved to see that Gideon was still playing in one of the bedrooms.

Aaron, Tuck, and Lance stood in unison but it was Lance who strode forward first. The moment he was within distance, he pulled his arm back and delivered a swift right cross to Jay's jaw. The man stumbled and leaned against the wall, his hand covering the point of impact. When he moved to straighten, Lance shoved him again.

Jay's gaze landed on Tuck. "You're a cop. Are you going to let him do that?"

Tuck raised an eyebrow. "Do what? I didn't see a thing."

Aaron looked from Jay to Serenity. "This is Gideon's father?"

She blinked, hardly believing her eyes. "Yeah." Her voice was barely above a whisper.

Aaron's jaw clenched and his eyes flashed. "Then I'd like to get in line behind Lance."

Tuck put his other hand on Aaron's shoulder. He maneuvered both men a few paces away from Jay. "Take a breather, you two."

Lance waved at Jay. "Are you kidding me? After what he's done to your sister?"

Tuck shot him a warning glare. "I'm aware of what he's done. And trust me, if it comes to it, I'll be the first to settle things." He turned his attention to Jay. "What're you doing here?"

Jay stood straight and dropped his hand from his jaw. "I heard about the tornado and the damage to the school." His gaze rested on Serenity. "I went by your house to make sure you and Gideon were okay and you weren't there. I figured you might come here. I didn't know what else to do."

Serenity's eyes narrowed. "You came by the house? How do you know where we live?" After being absent from their lives for so long, what made him think he had a right to ask about them?

Jay looked sheepish and rubbed the back of his neck with one hand. "I moved back to the area about six months ago." He took in all of the people watching him. "Can we go outside and talk?"

She shook her head as nearly everyone objected to his words and all eyes went to her. "No. We can talk right where we are."

Laurie stood. "I'll go keep Gideon company."

Serenity gave her a grateful smile. She certainly felt better knowing her son wasn't going to walk out in the middle of this particular conversation. When Laurie had disappeared, Serenity crossed her arms and sat on the arm on the couch. "Okay. Now talk."

He sighed resolutely. "I've been living in Kentucky — since before Gideon was born. I'm not proud of how I handled everything. My parents insisted we move in order to finish my senior year. I knew that was wrong but I had no backbone. I didn't know how to stand up to them." Regret etched itself in his face. "I agreed and we left. Serenity, a day didn't go by that I didn't wonder about him. Or think about you doing this all on your own."

"We weren't alone." Serenity's voice was strong and she stood, straightening her spine. "We had a lot of people who've been here for us since day one."

"I know. I'm glad." A mix of respect and longing flashed across his features. "I didn't realize how important that was until I met my wife." He held up his left hand complete with wedding ring. "I told Denise about everything and she's encouraged me to find you and make things right. It took me a while to get the courage to do that."

A dozen thoughts and emotions flowed through Serenity. She wanted to kick him out of the house and

191

tell him to never come back. She wanted to give him a good punch to the face like Lance had. But there was a shadow of the high school boy she'd known. She'd always thought he'd run out on them because that's what he wanted to do.

What if his parents really had made him leave to finish up his senior year? Even if that were true, he had the last five years to make up for it. But he hadn't come back — until now.

Jay must have been able to read her skepticism. "You have a whole list of reasons for not believing me. I get that. I'm not trying to find a way into your life. I want to do something to help provide for Gideon. I owe him that."

Pieces of a puzzle from the last couple of months came together in Serenity's mind. She squinted at him. "You're the reason Gideon got such a big scholarship to Hope Academy. And the backpack — was that you, too?"

Jay's ears turned red as he gave a single nod. "You weren't supposed to find out. I never wanted credit for it. I needed to do something for him — to make up for not helping before."

"And the hospital bill?"

Jay shrugged.

Lance and Aaron moved forward to flank Serenity. Lance pierced Jay with a glare. "If you didn't want credit for it, what are you doing here?"

~

Aaron had wanted to voice that question himself. As far as he was concerned, Jay's actions were just this side of stalking. Unless he was mistaken, the man had never contacted Serenity directly. Jay should have tried that first.

He resisted the need to reach out and touch Serenity's arm or hand.

Jay seemed to weigh his words before responding to Lance's question. "I found out about the tornado and the damage that the school had received. I wanted to make sure Serenity and Gideon were safe. That they'd made it out in one piece." He looked at Serenity, his eyes pleading. "That's the only reason I came here. I wouldn't have otherwise." He took a moment to gaze around the room. "It's been a long time since I set foot in this house."

Aaron caught Grams raising an eyebrow and planting her fists on her hips.

Serenity was chewing on her lower lip. She stared at Jay, as though she were trying to read his mind and discern whether he was telling the truth or not. "Gideon and I are fine. And we don't need your help."

"I know you don't. But you deserve it. I set up the scholarship because you wouldn't have accepted it from me otherwise. Am I wrong?"

She didn't hesitate. "No, you're not wrong."

"Then I ask you to take some time and think about it. I'm offering to pay for Gideon's tuition — with no obligation from you. If you don't want to see me again, I will respect your wishes. But it's my hope that someday, I might be able to introduce you, Gideon, and the rest of your family to my wife. Think about it."

He took a last look around him, handed Serenity a business card, and exited through the front door. Tuck closed it behind him.

Aaron was pretty sure they could have heard a feather hit the ground. He lightly touched Serenity's shoulder. "Are you okay?"

Serenity made a sound halfway between a laugh and a grunt. "I have no idea." She sought the faces of each of her family members and finally Aaron's as well. "I'm open to suggestions."

Patty led her to the couch and sat down next to her. "No one can decide anything for you. But no matter what, we'll be here to support you. Always."

Serenity's eyes got misty. She nodded slowly.

Grams lowered herself on the other side of Serenity. "I've gone through a lot in my collection of years and there's one thing I've come to learn. Forgiveness and second chances are gifts and they only come around so often. Sometimes we are lucky enough to receive such a gift. And sometimes, it's up to us to choose whether or not to give it."

Tuck disappeared down the hall for several minutes and returned with Laurie.

Gideon emerged as well, flopping onto Serenity's lap. She hugged him. "Being able to have Gideon attend Hope Academy has been an answer to prayer. In more ways than one. If it hadn't been for the scholarship Jay set up, none of that would've happened. We'd still be here. We wouldn't have met Aaron. And Gideon may not have said his first word." She released a slow lungful of air. "It's a chain of events that's pretty hard to ignore."

Aaron had always respected Serenity, but it was increased twofold tonight. For someone who didn't like to accept help and who'd had such a difficult time finding herself after what Jay did, it took a lot of courage to consider giving the guy a second chance. Even if he still wished he could deck him first.

Lexi winked at Serenity from across the room. "I'm

proud of you, little sister."

"Thanks." Serenity's voice was just above a whisper. "I love you. All of you."

With those last three words, her gaze settled on Aaron. He felt his heart expand as everyone around them faded into the background. He vaguely heard Grams suggest they go into the kitchen and find the cookies Laurie had brought. As the rest of the family cleared out of the room, Aaron moved to sit on the coffee table in front of her.

"Did you mean that?"

Her cheeks turned a pretty shade of pink, but there was no doubting the certainty in her expression. "I did."

"I'm glad." He reached for her hands and held them in his. "Because I love you, too." He stood, gently bringing Serenity to her feet. Every fiber of his being wanted to do what he could to protect this woman and her son. She'd only been in his life for two months and he couldn't imagine a day without her now. It was incredible how he'd never realized such a big part of himself was missing until Serenity made him whole.

"Aaron, what about your job?"

He cupped her face with his palms and smiled at her. "We'll figure it out." With his mouth inches from hers, he held her close. "Together." He kissed her, his lips caressing hers, as unspoken promises enveloped them both.

Chapter Twenty-Four

Right before the weekend ended, Serenity received an automated call from Hope Academy letting her know that classes would resume on Wednesday allowing the school time to finish repairs. She'd just set her cell phone down in the cup holder of the console of her car when Aaron's phone rang. "I'll bet I know who that is."

He tossed her a curious look and answered the call. "Well, at least we know you don't have to get Gideon ready for school tomorrow."

A Monday morning that didn't start quite as early as they usually did sounded good. But the message had only commented on classes. "I'm assuming I'm still supposed to show up for work, though." What was she going to do with Gideon?

"I'd come in tomorrow at your regular time and bring Gideon. At least you'll be checking in. Chances are, they'll send you home again until Wednesday."

"Probably so." Which would be for the best, given the situation. Though the thought of two days without pay didn't sit well with her. Even with Jay providing everything for Gideon's tuition — and she'd all but decided to accept his offer — money was still tight.

At least the call meant the electricity was probably back on. It was a relief to get back to their house and find it filled with cool air. Aaron helped them carry their things back in, including a relieved Kia. Gideon wasted no time in running to his room and settling in.

Serenity collapsed onto the futon and let her shoulder sink into the cushion. "What a crazy few days."

"Agreed." Aaron sat next to her. "I had a lot of fun getting to know your family. They're good people — you're fortunate."

"I know." She slipped her arm under his and laid her cheek against his shoulder. "They all seem to approve of you."

He chuckled. "I'm glad. I like all of them, too."

She nestled against his side when he put an arm around her shoulders. "Now we have to get Cynthia's policy figured out."

Silence fell over them. Serenity had tried to analyze different scenarios over the weekend and every time, she got overwhelmed. Eventually, she shoved all thoughts of it out of her head so she could enjoy the time with her family.

In a lot of ways, it felt like the end of a vacation. The last few days had been wonderful and mostly worry free. Now it was back to real life and all that waited for them. A heavy sigh escaped before she had time to rein it in.

Aaron kissed her hair. "We're going to take it one day at a time.

~

Most of the damage the tornado had caused seemed to be cleaned up. Aaron had expected to still see broken glass in the hallway, but there wasn't a shard to be found. Several windows were still covered by boards and he assumed that most of the reason for the delay in classes was because new window panes were going to be put in over the next two days.

Rushed footsteps approached from behind and soon Zane was walking with Aaron. "How was Kitner?"

"It was good. I got to meet everyone — including Gideon's dad. It was pretty crazy."

Zane's eyebrows shot up. "Wow. You jumped right into it, huh? I'm glad it went well."

"Her family's great. They're all protective of Serenity. She's the baby in the family. All I have to say is things had better work out between us or her brother and brother-in-law will hunt me down."

"Serious?"

"Oh yeah." Aaron laughed and Zane joined him, although Aaron was quite certain he spoke the truth. And that was all right. He respected both men for it. "Is Letty's classroom cleaned up?"

"They got those windows replaced on Friday. I think she's ready for the kids. She was going to go up to the office and see if Serenity needed her to watch Gideon today. We weren't sure if they were asking her to work or not."

"I don't know, either. She came in just in case. I can help Letty out, too. I think there are two or three people working at Hope who have children going here as well. We may be able to set up some short-term childcare." He ran through a checklist in his head as they stepped into his classroom. When the light switch was flipped on, Aaron's eyes went right to a note on his desk. "I doubt that's a welcome back letter."

Zane waited while Aaron read the words. "Cynthia wants me in her office as soon as I get this." It was impossible to ignore the dread building in his chest. "I'm pretty sure she saw me with Serenity during the storm."

"You know what?" Zane stood straight, his face a picture of annoyance. "There were bigger things that day than her blasted policy. Regardless of what happens, Letty and I are behind you."

Aaron crumpled the paper into a tiny ball and threw it into the wastebasket. It landed in the bottom without touching the rim. "I guess I may as well get this over with. Pray, huh?"

"Without a doubt."

He left his friend behind and worked his way towards Cynthia's office. *Okay, God. I don't have to tell you how badly I want to keep my job. But I want Serenity in my life even more. Give me the patience I need to deal with Cynthia and the right words to say.*

Cynthia was staring at the doorway when he entered as if she'd been waiting for him all morning. She motioned to the chair in front of her. "Have a seat, Mr. Randall." Her features were stony, giving no hint of what she was thinking. "I've spoken to both you and Ms. Chandler extensively about the policy regarding a student's parent. I have had suspicions it was being disregarded. I saw some evidence of that during the storm last week. Do you deny that's the case?"

What was he going to say? They'd been trying to keep it quiet up until now. But he wasn't going to lie.

They'd already decided that was something they wouldn't do. "No, I don't deny that."

"Do you intend to continue this relationship?"

"Yes." There was no doubt about it.

Cynthia sat in dramatic silence. "Then you leave me no choice. You, Mr. Randall, are terminated. I expect you to say your goodbyes and have your personal things removed from the classroom after your last class on Friday."

Aaron schooled his features and pinned her with a look. "What about Serenity. Is her job safe?"

She shrugged. "There's nothing written into the policy suggesting she should lose her employment."

That was all he needed to hear. He gave her a single nod. "See that it stays that way. I'll see you at the board meeting tomorrow." Without waiting for her response, he stood, pivoted, and walked out.

It wasn't until he was back in the hallway that the full impact of what Cynthia had done hit him in the chest. He no longer worked at Hope Academy. The children he loved to teach — he would never see most of them again. He swallowed hard.

And Serenity. She was going to beat herself up over this and that was the last thing he wanted her to do.

~

Serenity stared at Aaron, trying to process what she'd just heard. Disbelief morphed into anger and she used her foot to shove her chair away from the table in the breakroom. "This is insane. Even with all of her talk and threats, she seriously let you go?" How stupid was this? Aaron put his hands over hers and gave them a gentle squeeze. When she looked up at him, the last thing she expected was for him to be smiling. "What on earth do you find so funny?"

"Has anyone told you how adorable you are when you're angry?"

She wanted to get indignant or object, but the twinkle in his eye brought out a smile of her own. She ducked her head. "Stop. This is serious."

"I know it is. I already talked to Tuck and he's gathering as much information as he can about the people involved in the original dispute last spring." His expression grew somber. "We're going to go into that meeting as prepared as we possibly can be. I have every intention of fighting to get my job back. Between now and then, we pray."

"How can you be this calm?"

Aaron caught some strands of hair on her cheek and moved to tuck them behind her ear. "I'm not. I talk big." He winked. "What I do know is that I love you and that you and Gideon are the most important people in my life. By the end of Tuesday, one way or another, we'll know where we stand. We will figure this out."

Serenity remembered her conversation with Lexi and how she didn't use to think of the world as a glass half empty. She refused to do that now. Aaron was right. They might be in limbo for a few days, but then it'd be over. And regardless of whether Cynthia succeeded or not, she and Aaron would stand together. Serenity nodded. "You're right." She smiled. "We've got this."

They finished their lunch. Aaron kissed her briefly before they went their separate ways. When Serenity got back to the front office, Maggie greeted her with a wave.

"How was lunch?"

Serenity rolled her eyes. She thought about glossing over the whole mess but hesitated. When she first started working here, she had no idea what to make of Maggie. But over the last couple of months, she'd found in her not only a fun co-worker, but a friend as well. A friend she knew she could trust. She lowered her voice and told her what Cynthia said to Aaron.

"That woman is crazy. I figured she was all talk." Maggie slumped back in her chair, her eyes watery. "This place won't be the same without the Music Man. What about all the kids who look forward to seeing him every day?"

No, it wouldn't be the same. She knew, without a doubt, that Gideon would miss seeing him at school. Serenity stared at the desk, her mind going in all directions. An idea popped into her head and her eyes widened.

Maggie noticed, sitting up straight. "Ooohhh! Whatever it is, I want to help." She took in the room and lowered her voice. "What've you got?"

Chapter Twenty-Five

The moment Aaron walked into the conference room for the board meeting. There were more people sitting around the rectangular table than he'd expected. Along with the president and secretary, twelve of the eighteen members of the board were present as well. Aaron held tight to Serenity's hand and led her around to several empty chairs. Tuck followed closely behind them. They took a seat, the men on either side of Serenity.

The quarterly board meeting was open to the public, but apparently few outsiders attended.

Cynthia caught his eyes and shot him a look of disdain. Before she could glance away, he recognized a flash of worry as well. Aaron hadn't so much as said hello to her since he went to her office on Monday.

Zane and Letty were keeping Gideon with them during the meeting and Maggie had joined them. It felt good to know they had friends supporting them.

Aaron could feel Serenity's knee bouncing up and down under the table. He gently nudged her shoulder with his own. "Deep breaths. We're going to be okay."

She nodded quickly but said nothing.

Tuck reached over and massaged her neck a moment before clasping his hands on a file he'd put on the table in front of him.

The board meeting began and went through an extensive amount of time going over old business as well as items on the agenda. As the minutes ticked by, Aaron had to force himself to not shift nervously in his seat. This was it. An hour from now, he would know whether or not he got his job back.

One of the members of the board, Jean Thompson, finally asked, "Is there any new business we need to address today?"

Cynthia seemed happy to stand up and let everyone else know about the conflict she'd had a hand in. "Yes, I have a matter I'd like to inform the board about. This is concerning the new dating policy we put into effect a few months ago." She paused. "I'd spoken to both Mr. Randall and Ms. Chandler about the policy. I made certain they understood its meaning. Mr. Randall continued to pursue a relationship with Ms. Chandler. Since her son goes to this school and is one of the students that Mr. Randall works with, it was highly inappropriate. They consistently disregarded my concern."

She shot a haughty look in Aaron's direction. "In line with the policy, I released Mr. Randall from Hope Academy so that he can find employment elsewhere. I have given him until the end of the week to remove his belongings from the school." She regained her seat, appearing way too proud of herself.

Jean looked across the long table at Tuck, Serenity, and Aaron. "Can I assume that Mr. Randall is in attendance today?"

Aaron offered a firm nod. "I am."

"Have you begun the process of emptying your classroom?" Jean folded her hands together and watched him expectantly.

"No, I have not."

"And why is that?"

Aaron rolled his shoulders back. "Because I have every intention of getting my job reinstated." His voice came out clear and confident.

Jean hiked an eyebrow at him. "Would you care to explain?"

Despite the storm of nerves inside, he stood calmly. "I would, thank you. I believe the policy in general isn't appropriate. I understand that it's important to provide a safe environment for the kids attending this school, but my love life is simply not the school's business. I fail to see how it interferes with my ability to teach my students." He paused. "Yes, I was aware of the policy. I've loved working here with these amazing kids for the last five years. I hate the idea that I might not be coming back. But Ms. Chandler is important to me and I was forced to choose. When it came down to it, the decision was an easy one."

He sat down again, reaching for Serenity's hand and giving it a squeeze. She offered him a brief smile, lacing her fingers with his. He laid their joined hands on the table.

Jean focused her attention on Tuck. "I assume you are here on their behalf. Do you have anything to add?"

"Yes, ma'am." Tuck stood and opened the folder he'd brought with him. "My name's Kentucky Chandler. I'm an officer with the Kitner Police Department. Since learning about the policy and the threat of Mr. Randall losing his job, I thought I'd take the liberty of doing some investigating." He cleared his throat. "Before the event this last spring, the school had no issues with interpersonal disruptions. I asked about both individuals involved. The woman in the relationship was married to Cynthia's stepson." Tuck tipped his head towards Cynthia. "I mean no disrespect, ma'am."

Aaron exchanged a surprised look with Serenity. More notable was the fact that no one on the board seemed fazed.

Tuck continued. "It's my understanding that the stepson has donated a large sum of money to Hope Academy for years now. If I had to guess, after he found out about the affair, the last thing he wanted to do was to continue to support the school that started what eventually would result in the dissolution of his marriage. I don't know whether this dating policy was put in place to placate this large donor, or if it truly was to avoid something similar from happening again. Either way, it doesn't seem fair to make all of your employees pay for the bad life choices that one person made." He closed the file. "Thank you for your time."

Tuck sat down again and Aaron resisted the urge to shake his hand. He could have become a successful lawyer if he hadn't gone into law enforcement.

So Cynthia had been protecting her stepson all along. Or was the board going above and beyond to secure the continued donation from the man? Either way, the dating policy was clearly born from ulterior motives. Surely, now that the reasons were known outside of the board, they'd reconsider the whole thing.

Cynthia's face had turned a shade of crimson but Jean maintained her composure. "I appreciate your thoroughness, Officer Chandler. But what you've stated is nothing more than what the board is already aware of. The dating policy, while it might be unusual, was voted on by the board. Because it is currently in place, you are in violation of guidelines." She nodded to Cynthia. "You were given ample warnings. This school recognizes that you've done extraordinary work with the children here at Hope. But if we're going to maintain this policy, we have to enforce the consequences." She paused. "Is there anything else?

Aaron stared at her. That was it. They weren't even going to put it to a vote? Whatever amount of money the stepson was donating, it must have been an incredibly large sum. Until now, he really felt like things were going to work out. That the board would tell Cynthia she needed to get over herself. The realization that he was probably not going to get his job back hit him hard.

Serenity pushed her chair away from the table and stood. Aaron blinked at her. What was she doing?

"I do have something I'd like to say if I may."

Jean motioned for her to continue.

"I'm not just part of the relationship that seems to fly in the face of your policy. My son also attends this school. In the two months that he's been coming here, he's benefited greatly from all of the wonderful teachers and therapists, and that includes Aaron. Before beginning music therapy, my son was completely non-verbal. He spoke his first word last week." Her voice shook and she cleared her throat. "If it weren't for Aaron's ability to reach these kids in a way no one else can, I'm confident I would still be waiting to hear my son say Ma."

Her voice was stronger now and Aaron was completely captivated by her words as she continued.

"My son looks forward to his visits with the Music Man. And he's not the only one. The school is full of kids who will not only miss Aaron if he leaves, but who won't be receiving therapy that's helping to improve their lives."

Serenity turned then and went to the back of the room. She pulled on the door that led to the hall and held it open. People started pouring into the conference room. Aaron spotted Letty and Zane with Gideon between them. Maggie sent a wink his way. He recognized dozens of students and their parents. Several other teachers and therapists punctuated the crowd. They continued to file into the room until nearly all of the open space had been filled. Serenity returned to her spot at the table.

"There are thirty-eight families represented here. Each of them is ready to share how Aaron has helped their children. And they are more than willing to write up a complaint if his job is not reinstated."

Serenity put a hand on Aaron's shoulder and smiled at him. A lump formed in his throat and he tried to swallow past it. His eyes scanned all of the people who were there supporting him and got more nods of encouragement than he could count. *Wow, God. When You decide to do something, You go all out. Thank you.*

Jean seemed stunned and Cynthia's expression was unreadable. Around the table, there were multiple members of the board who were conversing among themselves.

Zane moved to the front of the group and motioned towards the people standing behind him. "Not only that, but many of Aaron's co-workers also consider him a friend. A member of the Hope Academy family. If you choose to let him go, you'll be losing more than your music therapist in the process."

The room erupted in applause. Aaron was clapped on the shoulders or back multiple times. He looked into Serenity's face. She grinned at him and took her seat. He leaned over and whispered into her ear. "How on earth did you pull this off? You never said a thing."

"I didn't want to get your hopes up." Her eyes sparkled. "You're a popular guy. You might as well get used to it."

Aaron chuckled. The back of his neck grew hot from all the attention.

Jean had been speaking with several other board members and finally cleared her throat. She held her hand high in an attempt to capture everyone's attention. "Excuse me, please." The room quieted down. "In light of the support from the parents and co-workers present, the board has recommended that two votes be taken. The first one is in regard to the dating policy that was established this last spring. All those in favor of removing the policy from Hope Academy's set guidelines, please raise your hands."

While not all of the board members did so, there was a clear majority in favor of it. "Very well. We will remove the policy from the guidelines." Applause broke out and Jean held another hand up to quiet everyone. "All of those in favor of allowing Mr. Randall to continue his job as the music therapist here at Hope Academy?"

Cynthia looked miserable and seemed to sink into her chair. She didn't raise her hand, though Aaron thought she might have been the only one. When her gaze met his, he recognized a flash of grudging respect.

Jean gave a nod. "With a majority of the board's approval, Mr. Randall, your job will be reinstated." She tipped her head towards Aaron. "If you should choose to accept, that is."

Aaron stood and turned to address his friends, students, and their families. "You're all like family to me. I'm not going anywhere."

The applause was deafening and Aaron was swept into the group as they exited the conference room and gravitated towards the front office. He was greeted by multiple parents who congratulated him, many sharing with him what kinds of progress they'd seen in their children thanks to him.

Friends and co-workers shook his hand, telling him they were glad they'd continue to see him at the school.

Aaron searched for Serenity and finally spotted her across the room with Zane, Letty, Maggie, and Tuck who was holding Gideon. More than anything, he wanted to go to her.

The room gradually emptied as everyone headed home for the evening. When he'd waved to the last parent, he was finally able to fully grasp what had happened. Emotions collided and he fought to keep control of them.

He turned and faced the six individuals who remained. Maggie squealed and ran towards him, her purple acrylic nails clacking together as she gave him a hug. "Congratulations, Music Man. Never doubt that you're appreciated by many." She gave him a wink.

Zane shook hands with Aaron and Letty followed up with a hug of her own. "It's nice when the good guys win," she said, her eyes filled with tears.

Aaron stretched a hand to Tuck. "I appreciate everything you did, man. Thank you."

Tuck gave his hand a firm shake. "You're welcome. I'm glad I could help." His face was serious but there was a sparkle in his eyes. "You take care of my sister and nephew and we'll call it even."

"You have my word." Aaron gave him a nod and finally turned to find Serenity watching him. Emotions chased each other across her face. Gideon let go of her hand and ran to him. Aaron dropped to his knees and enveloped the boy in a hug. "Hey, buddy. Thanks for being here. It meant a lot, you know that?" Gideon looked at him with a grin and ran back to Tuck.

Serenity chuckled. "Is it finally my turn to congratulate the man of the hour?"

~

Serenity's pulse raced when Aaron didn't hesitate. He strode forward and pulled her into his arms. He lifted her off the ground and swung her around several times before setting her back down on her feet.

"You are absolutely amazing, did you know that?"

Serenity shrugged. "I didn't do much. You're the one who's touched so many lives. And God brought everything together from there."

He kept a strong arm around her waist and pulled her close. He kissed her ear. "Thank you, sweetheart."

Serenity's heart filled to overflowing and words wouldn't come. She rested her head against his chest and hugged him tightly.

Tuck shook his head in mock concern. "Serenity, after all this mess, I wouldn't blame you if you changed your mind. If you get sick of seeing this guy every day, you know you're always welcome to come back to Kitner." He tried to keep back a smile but didn't quite succeed.

Serenity laughed when Aaron held a hand to his

heart as though he'd been wounded.

"I appreciate it, Tuck. But I don't think that'll be necessary." She caught her brother's nod of approval. The fact was, everyone at Hope Academy was becoming a second family. She planned to tell Jay she accepted his help with the tuition. She couldn't imagine a better school for Gideon.

"In that case, I say this calls for a celebration." Zane motioned to the doors leading out of the school. "Steak dinner on Aaron."

The group erupted in laughter as they exited the building.

Aaron kept hold of Serenity's hand and slowed until they were several paces behind everyone else. He stopped then and tugged her to face him.

His voice was just above a whisper. "I love you, Serenity. You and Gideon. You're my family."

Those words crashed through the last layer of control she'd had on her emotions all afternoon. Tears filled her eyes. "I love you, too."

He covered her lips with his in a kiss full of promise.

With a smile meant only for her, he took her hand in his and continued their trek across the parking lot.

Serenity marveled at how, only a few months ago, trading what she'd known for an uncertain future had scared her to no end. And now... Well, now she welcomed the change that loving Aaron brought into her life.

Lord, You always had faith in me even when I had so little in myself. Thank you for my son and my Music Man.

About the Author

Melanie D. Snitker has enjoyed writing fiction for as long as she can remember. She started out writing episodes of cartoon shows that she wanted to see as a child and her love of writing grew from there. She and her husband, Doug, live in Texas with their two children who keep their lives full of adventure, and two dogs who add a dash of mischief to the family dynamics. In her spare time, Melanie enjoys photography, reading, crochet, baking, archery, camping and hanging out with family and friends.

http://www.melaniedsnitker.com
https://twitter.com/MelanieDSnitker
https://www.facebook.com/melaniedsnitker

Acknowledgments

There are a lot of amazing people that helped to bring this book into existence.

Doug, your encouragement and support means the world to me. Oh, and let's not forget the Coke and editing chocolate. I love you!

Xander and Sydney, I always appreciate your patience when Mommy's writing. I love you both so much. I hope you know what an inspiration you are to me.

Crystal, I am so incredibly thankful to have you for a friend and a critique partner. There were many points in this process when I wanted to bang my head against a wall. Brainstorming, chatting, and laughing with you helped keep me sane. This has been a blast and I can't wait to do it again. Thanks, girl!

Franky, Victorine, Rachel, and Crystal, our critique group is simply awesome. You ladies rock!

I also want to thank my amazing beta readers: Steph, Debbie, Denny, Sandy, Faith, and Suzanne. Your time and suggestions are greatly appreciated. You are all a huge blessing to me!

Books by Melanie D. Snitker

Calming the Storm
(A Christian Romance Novel)

Love's Compass Series:
Finding Peace (Book 1)
Finding Hope (Book 2)
Finding Courage (Book 3)
Finding Faith (Book 4)

Made in the USA
San Bernardino, CA
04 February 2016